"A quick trip to the register office, a simple 'I do,' and you get to keep your house and I'll have somewhere safe for Nancie. You're her aunt-in-law—I don't imagine there would be any objection to you taking care of her."

But if Adam had imagined that May would fling her arms around him, proclaim him her savior—well, nothing had changed there, either.

Her eyes went from blank to blazing, like lightning out of a clear blue sky.

"That's not even remotely funny, Adam. Now, if you don't mind, I've got a houseful of guests who'll be expecting lunch in a couple of hours."

She was wearing shabby sweats, but she swept by him, head high, shoulders back. Despite her lack of inches and the fact that her puppy fat hadn't melted away but had instead evolved into soft curves, she was every inch the lady.

"May!"

She was at the door before she stopped, looked back at him.

"I'm serious," he said, a touch more sharply than he'd intended. "It would be a purely temporary arrangement. A marriage of convenience."

Dear Reader,

Welcome back to Maybridge, a town I created back in 1994. *SOS: Convenient Husband Required* is the sixth of my books to be set there (the full list is on my Web site), and if it existed it would undoubtedly be one of the most romantic places in Britain.

Along with the nearby city of Melchester, the villages of Little Hinton and Upper Haughton, I have created a world of my own from the places where I grew up. There's the river, the regenerated industrial areas and the vibrant arts and crafts center in a huge old coaching inn, with delightful boutiques around the cobbled courtyard.

May Coleridge comes from an old Maybridge family— the ones who lived in "the big house"—but she fell in love with Adam Wavell, who comes from the other end of the social scale, when they were both in high school. Now the tables are turned. Adam is rich and powerful, while May is about to lose everything. Adam can't quite escape his past, his family, or the memory of May's sweet kisses, no matter how hard he tries. Nor can he rid himself of the memory of his humiliation at the hand of May's grandfather. Or her coldness in the years since then.

He's sure that a temporary marriage of convenience will give him closure, but being close to May rekindles feelings he'd thought dead. Can a convenient marriage become something more?

Walk through the park with them and watch them fall in love all over again.

Warmest wishes

Liz

LIZ FIELDING

SOS: Convenient Husband Required

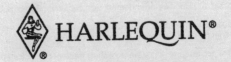

TORONTO • NEW YORK • LONDON
AMSTERDAM • PARIS • SYDNEY • HAMBURG
STOCKHOLM • ATHENS • TOKYO • MILAN • MADRID
PRAGUE • WARSAW • BUDAPEST • AUCKLAND

Recycling programs
for this product may
not exist in your area.

ISBN-13: 978-0-373-17670-0

SOS: CONVENIENT HUSBAND REQUIRED

First North American Publication 2010.

Liz Fielding was born with itchy feet. She made it to Zambia before her twenty-first birthday and, gathering her own special hero and a couple of children on the way, lived in Botswana, Kenya and Bahrain—with pauses for sightseeing pretty much everywhere in between. She finally came to a full stop in a tiny Welsh village cradled by misty hills, and these days mostly leaves her pen to do the traveling. When she's not sorting out the lives and loves of her characters she potters in the garden, reads her favorite authors and spends a lot of time wondering *What if...?* For news of upcoming books—and to sign up for her occasional newsletter—visit Liz's Web site at www.lizfielding.com.

For my patient, long-suffering husband, who unfailingly keeps his sense of humor through all the crises, the rubbish meals when the deadline escapes me, and makes me believe on those horrible days when the confidence falters. He is my hero.

CHAPTER ONE

MAY COLERIDGE stared blankly at the man sitting behind the desk, trying to make sense of what he'd told her.

Her grandfather's will had been simplicity itself. Apart from the bequests to local charities, everything had been left to his only living relative. Her.

Inheritance tax would mop up pretty much everything but the house itself. She'd always known that would happen, but Coleridge House was the only home she'd ever known and now, because of a clause in some centuries old will, she was about to lose that too.

'I don't understand,' she said, finally admitting defeat. 'Why didn't you tell me all this when you read Grandpa's will?'

'As you're no doubt aware,' Freddie Jennings explained with maddening pomposity—as if she hadn't known him since he'd been a kid with a runny nose at kindergarten— 'my great-uncle took care of your grandfather's legal affairs until he retired. He drew up his last will after the death of your mother—'

'That was nearly thirty years ago,' she protested.

He shrugged. 'Believe me, I'm as shocked as you are.'

'I doubt that. Jennings have been the Coleridge

family solicitor for generations,' she said. 'How could you not know about this?'

Freddie shifted uncomfortably in his chair. 'Some of the Coleridge archives were damaged during the floods a few years ago. It was only when I applied for probate that this particular condition of inheritance surfaced.'

May felt as if she'd stepped into quicksand and the ground that she was standing on, everything that had been certain, was disintegrating beneath her feet. She had been so sure that this was a mistake, that Freddie has got his knickers in a twist over nothing, but it wasn't nothing. It was everything.

Everything she'd known, everything she'd loved was being taken away from her...

'The last time this clause would have been relevant was when your great-grandfather died in 1944,' he continued, as if that mattered. 'Your grandfather would have been told of the condition then.'

'In 1944 my grandfather was a fourteen-year-old boy who'd just lost his father,' she snapped, momentarily losing her composure at his attempt to justify their incompetence. 'And, since he was married by the time he was twenty-three, it wouldn't have been an issue.' And by the time it had become one, the stroke that had incapacitated him had left huge holes in his memory and he hadn't been able to warn her. She swallowed as an aching lump formed in her throat, but she refused to let the tears fall. To weep. 'People got married so much younger back then,' she added.

'Back then, there wasn't any alternative.'

'No...'

Her mother had been a beneficiary of the feminist

movement, one of that newly liberated generation of women who'd abandoned the shackles of a patriarchal society and chosen her own path. *Motherhood without the bother of a man under her feet* was the way she'd put it in one of the many articles she'd written on the subject.

As for her, well, she'd had other priorities.

'You have to admit that it's outrageous, Freddie. Surely I can challenge it?'

'I'd have to take Counsel's opinion and even if you went to court there is a problem.'

'I think we are both agreed that I have a problem.'

He waited, but she shook her head. Snapping at Freddie wasn't going to help. 'Tell me.'

'There can be no doubt that this restriction on inheritance would have been explained to your grandfather on each of the occasions when he rewrote his will. After his marriage, the birth of your mother, the death of your grandmother. He could have take steps then to have this restriction removed. He chose to let it stand.'

'Why? Why would he do that?'

Freddie shrugged. 'Maybe because it was part of family tradition. Maybe because his father had left it in place. I would have advised removal but my great-uncle, your grandfather came from a different age. They saw things differently.'

'Even so—'

'He had three opportunities to remove the entailment and the Crown would argue that it was clearly his wish to let it stand. Counsel would doubtless counter that if he hadn't had a stroke, had realised the situation you were in, he would have changed it,' Freddie said in an attempt to comfort her.

'If he hadn't had a stroke I would be married to

Michael Linton,' she replied. *Safely married.* That was what he used to say. Not like her mother…

'I'm sorry, May. The only guarantee I can give is that whichever way it went the costs would be heavy and, as you are aware, there's no money in the estate to cover them.'

'You're saying that I'd lose the house anyway,' she said dully. 'That whatever I do I lose.'

'The only people who ever win in a situation like this are the lawyers,' he admitted. 'Hopefully, you'll be able to realise enough from the sale of the house contents, once the inheritance tax is paid, to provide funds for a flat or even a small house.'

'They want inheritance tax *and* the house?'

'The two are entirely separate.'

She shook her head, still unable to believe this was happening. 'If it was going to some deserving charity I could live with it, but to have my home sucked into the Government coffers…' Words failed her.

'Your ancestor's will was written at the beginning of the nineteenth century. The country was at war. He was a patriot.'

'Oh, please! It was nothing but an arm twisted up the back of a philandering son. Settle down and get on with producing the next generation or I'll cut you off without a shilling.'

'Maybe. But it was added as an entailment to the estate and no one has ever challenged it. There's still just time, May. You could get married.'

'Is that an offer?'

'Unfortunately, bigamy would not satisfy the legal requirements.'

Freddie Jennings had a sense of humour? Who knew?

'You're not seeing anyone?' he asked hopefully.

She shook her head. There had only ever been one boy, man, who'd ever lit a fire in her heart, her body…

'Between nursing Grandpa and running my own business, I'm afraid there hasn't been a lot of time to "see" anyone,' she said.

'There's not even a friend who'd be prepared to go through the motions?'

'I'm all out of unattached men at the moment,' she replied. 'Well, there is Jed Atkins who does a bit for me in the garden now and then,' she said, her grip on reality beginning to slip. 'He's in his seventies, but pretty lively and I'd have to fight off the competition.'

'The competition?'

'He's very much in demand with the ladies at the Darby and Joan club, so I'm told.'

'May…' he cautioned as she began to laugh, but the situation was unreal. How could he expect her to take it seriously? 'I think I'd better take you home.'

'I don't suppose you have any clients in urgent need of a marriage of convenience so that they can stay in the country?' she asked as he ushered her from his office, clearly afraid that she was going to become hysterical.

He needn't have worried. She was a Coleridge. Mary Louise Coleridge of Coleridge House. Brought up to serve the community, behave impeccably on all occasions, do the right thing even when your heart was breaking.

She wasn't about to become hysterical just because Freddie Jennings had told her she was about to lose everything.

'But if you are considering something along those

lines,' he warned as he held the car door for her, 'please make sure he signs a pre-nuptial agreement or you're going to have to pay dearly to get rid of him.'

'Make that a lose/lose/lose situation,' she said. Then, taking a step back, 'Actually, I'd rather walk home. I need some fresh air.'

He said something but she was already walking away. She needed to be on her own. Needed to think.

Without Coleridge House, she would not only lose her home, but her livelihood. As would Harriet Robson, her grandfather's housekeeper for more than thirty years and the nearest thing to a mother she'd ever known.

She'd have to find a job. Somewhere to live. Or, of course, a husband.

She bought the early edition of the local newspaper from the stand by the park gates to look at the sits vac and property columns. What a joke. There were no jobs for a woman weeks away from her thirtieth birthday who didn't have a degree or even a typing certificate to her name. And the price of property in Maybridge was staggering. The lonely hearts column was a boom area, though, and, with a valuable house as an incentive, a husband might prove the easiest of the three to find. But, with three weeks until her birthday, even that was going to be a tough ask.

Adam Wavell looked from the sleeping infant tucked into the pink nest of her buggy to the note in his hand.

Sorry, sorry, sorry. I know I should have told you about Nancie, but you'd have shouted at me...

Shouted at her. Shouted at her! Of course he would have shouted at her, for all the good it had ever done.

'Problem?'

'You could say that.' For the first time since he'd employed Jake Edwards as his PA, he regretted not choosing one of the equally qualified women who'd applied for the job, any one of whom would by now have been clucking and cooing over the infant. Taking charge and leaving him to get on with running his company. 'My sister is having a crisis.'

'I didn't know you had a sister.'

No. He'd worked hard to distance himself from his family.

'Saffy. She lives in France,' he said.

Maybe. It had taken only one call to discover that she'd sublet the apartment he'd leased for her months ago. Presumably she was living off the proceeds of the rent since she hadn't asked him for money. Yet.

Presumably she'd moved in with the baby's father, a relationship that she hadn't chosen to share with him and had now, presumably, hit the skids.

Her occasional phone calls could have come from anywhere and any suggestion that he was cross-examining her about what she was doing, who she was seeing only resulted in longer gaps between them. It was her life and while she seemed happy he didn't pry. At twenty-nine, she was old enough to have grown out of her wildness and settled down. Clearly, he thought as he reread the letter, he'd been fooling himself.

I've got myself into some real trouble, Adam...

Trouble. Nothing new there, then. She'd made a career of it.

Michel's family set their bloodhounds on me. They've found out all the trouble I was in as a kid, the shoplifting, the drugs and they've used it to turn him against me. He's got a court order to stop me taking Nancie out of France and he's going to take her away from me...

No. That wasn't right. She'd been clean for years... Or was he still kidding himself?

A friend smuggled us out of France but I can't hide with a baby so I'm leaving her with you...

Smuggled her out of France. Ignored a court order. Deprived a father of access to his child. Just how many felonies did that involve? All of which he was now an accessory to.

Terrific.

One minute he'd been sitting in his boardroom, discussing the final touches to the biggest deal in his career, the next he was having his life sabotaged—not for the first time—by his family.

I'm going to disappear for a while...

No surprise there. His little sister had made a career of running away and leaving someone else to pick up the pieces. She'd dropped out, run away, used drugs and alcohol in a desperate attempt to shut out all the bad stuff. Following the example of their useless parents. Making a bad situation worse.

He'd thought his sister had finally got herself together, was enjoying some small success as a model. Or maybe that was what he'd wanted to believe.

Don't, whatever you do, call a nanny agency. They'll want all kinds of information and, once it's on record, Nancie's daddy will be able to trace her...

Good grief, who was the father of this child? Was his sister in danger?

Guilt overwhelmed those first feelings of anger, frustration. He had to find her, somehow make this right, but, as the baby stirred, whimpered, he had a more urgent problem.

Saffy had managed to get her into his office without anyone noticing her—time for a shake-up in security— but that would have to wait. His first priority was to get the baby out of the building before she started screaming and his family history became the subject of the kind of gossip that had made his—and Saffy's—youth a misery.

'Do you want me to call an agency?' Jake asked.

'An agency?'

'For a nanny?'

'Yes... No...'

Even if Saffy's fears were nothing but unfounded neurosis he didn't have anywhere to put a nanny. He didn't even have a separate bedroom in his apartment, only a sleeping gallery reached by a spiral staircase.

It was no place for a baby, he thought as he stared at the PS Saffy had scribbled at the end of the crumpled and tear-stained note.

Ask May. She'll help.

She'd underlined the words twice.
May. May Coleridge.
He crushed the letter in his hand.
He hadn't spoken to May Coleridge since he was eighteen. She and Saffy had been in the same class at school and, while they hadn't been friends—the likes of the Wavells had not been welcome at Coleridge House, as he'd discovered to his cost—at least not in the giggly girls, shopping, clubbing sense of the word, there had been some connection between them that he'd never been able to fathom.

But then that was probably what people had thought about him and May.

But while the thought of the untouchable Miss Coleridge changing the nappy of a Wavell baby might put a shine on his day, the woman had made an art form of treating him as if he were invisible.

Even on those social occasions when they found themselves face to face, there was no eye contact. Only icy civility.

'Is there anything I can do?'

He shook his head. There was nothing anyone could do. His family was, always had been, his problem, but it was a mess he wanted out of his office. Now.

'Follow up on the points raised at the meeting, Jake.' He looked at the crumpled sheet of paper in his hand, then folded it and stuffed it in his shirt pocket.

Unhooked his jacket from the back of his chair. 'Keep me posted about any problems. I'm going home.'

It took a kitten to drag May out of her dark thoughts.

Her first reaction to the news that she was about to lose her home had been to rush back to its shabby comfort—no matter how illusory that comfort might be—while she came to terms with the fact that, having lost the last surviving member of her family, she was now going to lose everything else. Her home. Her business. Her future.

Once home, however, there would be no time for such indulgence. She had little enough time to unravel the life she'd made for herself. To wind down a business she'd fallen into almost by accident and, over the last few years, built into something that had given her something of her own, something to live for.

Worst of all, she'd have to tell Robbie.

Give notice to Patsy and the other women who worked for a few hours a week helping with the cleaning, the cooking and who relied on that small amount of money to help them pay their bills.

There'd be no time to spare for the luxury of grieving for the loss of their support, friendship. Her birthday was less than a month away. *The* birthday. The one with a big fat zero on the end.

Yesterday that hadn't bothered her. She'd never understood why anyone would want to stop the clock at 'twenty-nine'.

Today, if some fairy godmother were to appear and offer her three wishes, that would be number one on the list. Well, maybe not number one...

But, while fairy godmothers were pure fantasy, her

date of birth was a fact that she could not deny and, by the time she'd reached the last park bench before home, the one overlooking the lake that had once been part of the parkland surrounding Coleridge House, her legs had been shaking so much that she'd been forced to stop.

Once there, she'd been unable to find the will to move again. It was a sheltered spot, a sun trap and, despite the fact that it was the first week in November, pleasantly warm. And while she sat on this park bench she was still Miss Mary Louise Coleridge of Coleridge House. Someone to be respected.

Her place in the town, the invitations to sit on charitable committees were part of her life. Looked at in the cold light of day, it was obvious that it wasn't her they wanted, it was the Coleridge name to lend lustre to their endeavours. And Coleridge House.

No one would come knocking when she didn't have a grand room where they could hold their meetings, with a good lunch thrown in. An elegant, if fading house with a large garden in which to hold their 'events'.

It was the plaintive mewing of a kitten in distress that finally broke through these dark thoughts. It took her a moment to locate the scrap of orange fur clinging to the branch of a huge old beech tree set well back from the path.

'Oh, sweetie, how on earth did you get up there?'

Since the only reply was an even more desperate mew, she got to her feet and went closer.

'Come on. You can do it,' she cooed, standing beneath it, hoping to coax it back down the long sloping branch that came nearly to the ground. It edged further up the branch.

She looked around, hoping for someone tall enough

to reach up and grab it but there wasn't a soul in sight. Finally, when it became clear that there wasn't anything else for it, she took off her jacket, kicked off her shoes and, skirting a muddy puddle, she caught hold of the branch, found a firm foothold and pulled herself up.

Bitterly regretting that he'd taken advantage of the unseasonably fine weather to walk in to the office, Adam escaped the building via his private lift to the car park. He'd hoped to pick up a taxi at the rank on the corner but there were none waiting and he crossed the road to the park. It was a slightly longer way home, but there was less chance of being seen by anyone he knew.

Oblivious to the beauty of the autumn morning, he steered the buggy with one hand, using the other to call up anyone who might have a clue where Saffy was heading for.

His first action on finding Nancie had been to try her mother's mobile but, unsurprisingly, it was switched off. He'd left a message on her voicemail, asking her to ring him, but didn't hold out much hope of that.

Ten minutes later, the only thing he knew for certain was that he knew nothing. The new tenants of the apartment, her agent—make that ex-agent—even her old flatmate denied any knowledge of where she was, or of Michel, and he had no idea who her friends were, even supposing they'd tell him anything.

Actually, he thought, looking at the baby, it wasn't true that he knew nothing.

While the movement of the buggy had, for the moment, lulled her back to sleep, he was absolutely sure that very soon she would be demanding to be fed or changed.

Ask May. She'll help.

Ahead of him, the tall red-brick barley twist chimneys of Coleridge House stood high above the trees. For years he'd avoided this part of the park, walked double the distance rather than pass the house. Just seeing those chimneys had made him feel inadequate, worthless.

These days, he could buy and sell the Coleridges, and yet it was still there. Their superiority and the taint of who he was.

Asking her for help stuck deep in his craw, but the one thing about May Coleridge was that she wouldn't ask questions. She knew Saffy. Knew him.

He called Enquiries for her number but it was unlisted. No surprise there, but maybe it was just as well.

It had been a very long time since he'd taken her some broken creature to be nursed back to health, but he knew she'd find it a lot harder to say no face to face. If he put Nancie into her arms.

It is not high, May told herself as she set her foot firmly on the tree. All she had to do was haul herself up onto the branch and crawl along it. No problem…

Easy enough to say when she was safely on the ground.

Standing beneath the branch and looking up, it had seemed no distance at all. The important thing, she reminded herself, was not to look down but keep her eye on the goal.

'What on earth are you doing up there, Mouse?'

Sherbet dabs!

As her knee slipped, tearing her tights, she wondered how much worse this day could get. The advantage that she didn't have to look down to see who was beneath her—only one person had ever called her Mouse—was completely lost on her.

'What do you think I'm doing?' she asked through gritted teeth. 'Checking the view?'

'You should be able to see Melchester Castle from up there,' he replied, as if she'd been serious. 'You'll have to look a little further to your left, though.'

She was in enough trouble simply looking ahead. She'd never been good with heights—something she only ever seemed to remember when she was too far off the ground to change her mind.

'Why don't you come up and point it out to me?' she gasped.

'I would be happy to,' he replied, 'but that branch doesn't look as if it could support both of us.'

He was right. It was creaking ominously as she attempted to edge closer to the kitten which, despite her best efforts not to frighten it further, was backing off, a spitting, frightened orange ball of fur.

It was far too late to wish she'd stuck to looking helpless at ground level. She'd realised at a very early age that the pathetic, *Where's a big strong man to help me?* routine was never going to work for her—she wasn't blonde enough, thin enough, pretty enough—and had learned to get on and do it herself.

It was plunging in without a thought for the consequences that had earned her the mocking nickname 'Mouse', short for 'Danger Mouse', bestowed on her by Adam Wavell when she was a chubby teen and he was a mocking, nerdy, glasses-wearing sixth-former at the local high school.

Her knee slipped a second time and a gasp from

below warned her that Adam wasn't the only one
with a worm's eye view of her underwear. A quick
blink confirmed that her antics were beginning to
attract an audience of mid-morning dog-walkers,
older children on their autumn break and shoppers
taking the scenic route into the town centre—just too
late to be of help.

Then a click, followed by several more as the idea
caught on, warned her that someone had taken a photograph using their mobile phone. Terrific. She was
going to be in tomorrow's edition of the *Maybridge
Observer* for sure; worse, she'd be on *YouTube* by lunch
time.

She had no one to blame but herself, she reminded
herself, making a firm resolution that the next time she
spotted an animal in distress she'd call the RSPCA and
leave it to them. That wasn't going to help her now,
though, and the sooner she grabbed the kitten and
returned to earth the better.

'Here, puss,' she coaxed desperately, but its only
response was to hiss at her and edge further along the
branch. Muttering under her breath, she went after it. The
kitten had the advantage. Unlike her, it weighed nothing
and, as the branch thinned and began to bend noticeably
beneath her, she made a desperate lunge, earning herself
a cheer from the crowd as she managed to finally grab
it. The kitten ungratefully sank its teeth into her thumb.

'Pass it down,' Adam said, his arms raised to take
it from her.

Easier said than done. In its terror, it had dug its
needle claws in, clinging to her hand as desperately as
it had clung to the branch.

'You'll have to unhook me. Don't let it go!' she

warned as she lowered it towards him. She was considerably higher now and she had to lean down a long way so that he could detach the little creature with the minimum of damage to her skin.

It was a mistake.

While she'd been focused on the kitten everything had been all right, but that last desperate lunge had sent everything spinning and, before she could utter so much as a *fudge balls*, she lost her balance and slithered off the branch.

Adam, standing directly beneath her, had no time to avoid a direct hit. They both went down in a heap, the fall driving the breath from her body, which was probably a good thing since there was no item in her handmade confectionery range that came even close to matching her mortification. But then embarrassment was her default reaction whenever she was within a hundred feet of the man.

'You don't change, Mouse,' he said as she struggled to catch her breath.

Not much chance of that while she was lying on top of him, his breath warm against her cheek, his heart pounding beneath her hand, his arm, flung out in an attempt to catch her—or, more likely, defend himself—tight around her. The stuff of her most private dreams, if she discounted the fact that it had been raining all week and they were sprawled in the muddy puddle she had taken such pains to avoid.

'You always did act first, think later,' he said. 'Rushing to the aid of some poor creature in distress and getting wet, muddy or both for your pains.'

'While you,' she gasped, 'always turned up too late to do anything but stand on the sidelines, laughing at me,' she replied furiously. It was untrue and unfair, but all she wanted right at that moment was to vanish into thin air.

'You have to admit you were always great entertainment value.'

'If you like clowns,' she muttered, remembering all too vividly the occasion when she'd scrambled onto the school roof in a thunderstorm to rescue a bird trapped in the guttering and in danger of drowning, concern driving her chubby arms and legs as she'd shinned up the down pipe.

Up had never been a problem.

He'd stood below her then, the water flattening his thick dark hair, rain pouring down his face, grinning even as he'd taken the bird from her. But then, realising that she was too terrified to move, he'd taken off his glasses and climbed up to rescue her.

Not that she'd thanked him.

She'd been too busy yelling at him for letting the bird go before she could wrap it up and take it home to join the rest of her rescue family.

It was only when she was back on terra firma that her breathing had gone to pot and he'd delivered her to the school nurse, convinced she was having an asthma attack. And she had been too mortified—and breathless—to deny it.

He was right. Nothing had changed. She might be less than a month away from her thirtieth birthday, a woman of substance, respected for her charity work, running her own business, but inside she was still the overweight and socially inept teen being noticed by a boy she had the most painful crush on. Brilliant but geeky with the family from hell. Another outsider.

Well, he wasn't an outsider any more. He'd used his

brains to good effect and was now the most successful man not just in Maybridge, but just about anywhere and had exchanged the hideous flat in the concrete acres of a sink estate where he'd been brought up for the luxury of a loft on the quays.

She quickly disentangled herself, clambered to her feet. He followed with far more grace.

'Are you all right?' he asked. 'No bones broken?'

'I'm fine,' she said, ignoring the pain in her elbow where it had hit the ground. 'You?' she asked out of politeness.

She could see for herself that he was absolutely fine. More than fine. The glasses had disappeared years ago, along with the bad hair, bad clothes. He'd never be muscular, but he'd filled out as he'd matured, his shoulders had broadened and these days were clad in the finest bespoke tailoring.

He wasn't just fine, but gorgeous. Mouth-wateringly scrumptious, in fact. The chocolate nut fudge of maleness. And these days he had all the female attention he could handle if the gossip magazines were anything to judge by.

'At least you managed to hang onto the kitten,' she added, belatedly clutching the protective cloak of superiority about her.

The one thing she knew would make him keep his distance.

'I take no credit. The kitten is hanging onto me.'

'What?' She saw the blood seeping from the needle wounds in his hand and everything else flew out of the window. 'Oh, good grief, you're bleeding.'

'It's a hazard I expect whenever I'm within striking

distance of you. Although on this occasion you haven't escaped unscathed, either,' he said.

She physically jumped as he took her own hand in his, turning it over so that she could see the tiny pinpricks of blood mingling with the mud. And undoing all her efforts to regain control of her breathing. He looked up.

'Where's your bag?' he asked. 'Have you got your inhaler?'

Thankfully, it had never occurred to him that his presence was the major cause of her problems with breathing.

'I'm fine,' she snapped.

For heaven's sake, she was nearly thirty. She should be so over the cringing embarrassment that nearly crippled her whenever Adam Wavell was in the same room.

'Come on,' he said, 'I'll walk you home.'

'There's no need,' she protested.

'There's every need. And this time, instead of getting punished for my good deed, I'm going to claim my reward.'

'Reward?' Her mouth dried. In fairy tales that would be a kiss... 'Superheroes never hang around for a reward,' she said scornfully as she wrapped the struggling kitten in her jacket.

'You're the superhero, Danger Mouse,' he reminded her, a teasing glint in his eyes that brought back the precious time when they'd been friends. 'I'm no more than the trusty sidekick who turns up in the nick of time to get you out of a jam.'

'Just once in a while you could try turning up in time to prevent me from getting into one,' she snapped.

'Now where would be the fun in that?' he asked, and

it took all her self-control to keep her face from breaking out into a foolish smile.

'Do you really think I want to be on the front page of the *Maybridge Observer* with my knickers on show?' she enquired sharply. Then, as the teasing sparkle went out of his eyes, 'Don't worry. I'm sure I'll survive the indignity.'

'Having seen your indignity for myself, I can assure you that tomorrow's paper will be a sell-out,' he replied. She was still struggling with a response to that when he added, 'And if they can tear their eyes away from all that lace, the kitten's owners might recognise their stray.'

'One can live in hopes,' she replied stiffly.

She shook her head, then, realising that, no matter how much she wanted to run and hide, she couldn't ignore the fact that because of her he was not only bloody but his hand-stitched suit was covered in mud.

'I suppose you'd better come back to the house and get cleaned up,' she said.

'If that's an offer to hose me down in the yard, I'll pass.'

For a moment their eyes met as they both remembered that hideous moment when he'd come to the house with a bunch of red roses that must have cost him a fortune and her grandfather had turned a garden hose on him, soaking him to the skin.

'Don't be ridiculous,' she said, her insides curling up with embarrassment, killing stone dead the little heart-lift as he'd slipped so easily into teasing her the way he'd done when they were friends.

She picked up her shoes, her bag, reassembling her armour. But she wasn't able to look him in the eye as she added distantly, 'Robbie will take care of you in the kitchen.'

'The kitchen? Well, that will be further than I've ever got before. But actually it was you I was coming to see.'

She balanced her belongings, then, with studied carelessness, as if she had only then registered what he'd said, 'See?' she asked, doing her best to ignore the way her heart rate had suddenly picked up. 'Why on earth would you be coming to see me?'

He didn't answer but instead used his toe to release the brake on a baby buggy that was standing a few feet away on the path. The buggy that she had assumed belonged to a woman, bundled up in a thick coat and headscarf, who'd been holding onto the handle, crooning to the baby.

CHAPTER TWO

'ADAM? What are you doing?'

'Interesting question. Mouse, meet Nancie.'

'Nancy?'

'With an i and an e. Spelling never was Saffy's strong point.'

Saffy Wavell's strong points had been so striking she'd never given a fig for spelling or anything much else. Long raven-black hair, a figure that appeared to be both ethereal and sensual, she'd been a boy magnet since she hit puberty. And in trouble ever since. But a baby...

'She's Saffy's baby? That's wonderful news.' She began to smile. 'I'm so happy for her.' The sleeping baby was nestled beneath a pink lace-bedecked comforter. 'She's beautiful.'

'Is she?'

He leaned forward for a closer look, as if it hadn't occurred to him, but May stopped, struck by what he'd just done.

'You just left her,' she said, a chill rippling through her. 'She's Saffy's precious baby and you just abandoned her on the footpath to come and gawp at me? What on earth were you thinking, Adam?'

He looked back then, frowning; he stopped too, clearly catching from her tone that a grin would be a mistake.

'I was thinking that you were in trouble and needed a hand.'

'Idiot!' For a moment there she'd been swept away by the sight of a powerful man taking care of a tiny infant. 'I'm not a child. I could have managed.'

'Well, thanks—'

'Don't go getting all offended on me, Adam Wavell,' she snapped, cutting him off. 'While you were doing your Galahad act, anyone could have walked off with her.'

'What?' Then, realising what she was saying, he let go of the handle, rubbed his hands over his face, muttered something under his breath. 'You're right. I am an idiot. I didn't think.' Then, looking at the baby, 'I'm way out of my depth here.'

'Really? So let me guess,' May said, less than amused; he was overdoing it with the 'idiot'. 'Your reason for dropping in for the first time in years wouldn't have anything to do with your sudden need for a babysitter?'

'Thanks, May. Saffy said you'd help.'

'She said that?' She looked at the baby. All pink and cute and helpless. No! She would not be manipulated! She was in no position to take on anyone else's problems right now. She had more than enough of her own. 'I was stating the obvious, not offering my services,' she said as he began to walk on as if it was a done deal. 'Where is Saffy?'

'She's away,' he said. 'Taking a break. She's left Nancie in my care.'

'Good luck with that,' she said. 'But it's no use

coming to me for help. I know absolutely nothing about babies.'

'You've already proved you know more than me. Besides, you're a woman.' Clearly he wasn't taking her refusal seriously, which was some nerve considering he hadn't spoken to her unless forced to in the last ten years. 'I thought it came hard-wired with the X chromosome?'

'That is an outrageous thing to say,' she declared, ignoring the way her arms were aching to pick up the baby, hold her, tell her that she wouldn't allow anything bad to happen to her. Ever. Just as she'd once told her mother.

She already had the kitten. In all probability, that was all she'd ever have. Ten years from now, she'd be the desperate woman peering into other people's prams…

'Is it?' he asked, all innocence.

'You know it is.'

'Maybe if you thought of Nancie as one of those helpless creatures you were always taking in when you were a kid it would help?' He touched a finger to the kitten's orange head, suggesting that nothing had changed. 'They always seemed to thrive.'

'Nancie,' she said, ignoring what she assumed he thought was flattery, 'is not an injured bird, stray dog or frightened kitten.'

'The principle is the same. Keep them warm, dry and fed.'

'Well, there you are,' she said. 'You know all the moves. You don't need me.'

'On the contrary. I've got a company to run. I'm flying to South America tomorrow—'

'South America?'

'Venezuela first, then on to Brazil and finally

Samindera. Unless you read the financial pages, you would have missed the story. I doubt it made the social pages,' he said.

'Samindera,' she repeated with a little jolt of concern. 'Isn't that the place where they have all the coups?'

'But grow some of the finest coffee in the world.' One corner of his mouth lifted into a sardonic smile that, unlike the rest of him, hadn't changed one bit.

'Well, that's impressive,' she said, trying not to remember how it had felt against her own trembling lips. The heady rush as a repressed desire found an urgent response… 'But you're not the only one with a business to run.' Hers might be little more than a cottage industry, nothing like his international money generator that had turned him from zero to a Maybridge hero, but it meant a great deal to her. Not that she'd have it for much longer.

Forget Adam, his baby niece, she had to get home, tell Robbie the bad news, start making plans. Somehow build a life from nothing.

Just as Adam had done…

'I've got a world of trouble without adding a baby to the mix,' she said, not wanting to think about Adam. Then, before he could ask her what kind of trouble, 'I thought Saffy was living in Paris. Working as a model? The last I heard from her, she was doing really well.'

'She kept in touch with you?' Then, before she could answer, 'Why are you walking barefoot, May?'

She stared at him, aware that he'd said something he regretted, had deliberately changed the subject, then, as he met her gaze, challenging her to go there, she looked down at her torn tights, mud soaked skirt, dirty legs and feet.

'My feet are muddy. I've already ruined my good black suit…' the one she'd be needing for job interviews, assuming anyone was that interested in someone who hadn't been to university, had no qualifications '…I'm not about to spoil a decent pair of shoes, too.'

As she stepped on a tiny stone and winced, he took her by the arm, easing her off the path and she froze.

'The grass will be softer to walk on,' he said, immediately releasing her, but not before a betraying shiver of gooseflesh raced through her.

Assuming that she was cold, he removed his jacket, placed it around her shoulders. It swallowed her up, wrapping her in the warmth from his body.

'I'm covered in mud,' she protested, using her free hand to try and shake it off. Wincing again as a pain shot through her elbow. 'It'll get all over the lining.'

He stopped her, easing the jacket back onto her shoulder, then holding it in place around her. 'You're cold,' he said, looking down at her, 'and I don't think this suit will be going anywhere until it's been cleaned, do you?'

Avoiding his eyes, she glanced down at his expensively tailored trousers, but it wasn't the mud that made her breath catch in her throat. He'd always been tall but now the rest of him had caught up and those long legs, narrow hips were designed to make a woman swoon.

'No!' she said, making a move so that he was forced to turn away. 'You'd better send me the cleaning bill.'

'It's your time I need, May. Your help. Not your money.'

He needed her. Words which, as a teenager, she'd lived to hear. Words that, when he shouted them for all the world to hear, had broken her heart.

'It's impossible right now.'

'I heard about your grandfather,' he said, apparently assuming it was grief that made her so disobliging.

'Really?' she said.

'It said in the *Post* that the funeral was private.'

'It was.' She couldn't have borne the great and good making a show of it. And why would Adam have come to pray over the remains of a man who'd treated him like something unpleasant he'd stepped in? 'But there's going to be a memorial service. He was generous with his legacies and I imagine the charities he supported are hoping that a showy civic send-off will encourage new donors to open their wallets. I'm sure you'll get an invitation to that.' Before he could answer, she shook her head. 'I'm sorry. That was a horrible thing to say.'

But few had done more than pay duty visits after a massive stroke had left her grandpa partially paralysed, confused, with great holes in his memory. Not that he would have wanted them to see him that way.

'He hated being helpless, Adam. Not being able to remember.'

'He was a formidable man. You must miss him.'

'I lost him a long time ago.' Long before his memory had gone.

'So, what happens now?' Adam asked, after a moment of silence during which they'd both remembered the man they knew. 'Will you sell the house? It needs work, I imagine, but the location would make it ideal for company offices.'

'No!' Her response was instinctive. She knew it was too close to the town, didn't have enough land these days to attract a private buyer with that kind of money to spend, but the thought of her home being turned into some company's fancy corporate headquarters—or, more likely, government offices—was too much to bear.

'Maybe a hotel or a nursing home,' he said, apparently understanding her reaction and attempting to soften the blow. 'You'd get a good price for it.'

'No doubt, but I won't be selling.'

'No? Are you booked solid into the foreseeable future with your painters, garden designers and flower arrangers?'

She glanced at him, surprised that he knew about the one-day and residential special interest courses she ran in the converted stable block.

'Your programme flyer is on the staff noticeboard at the office.'

'Oh.' She'd walked around the town one Sunday stuffing them through letterboxes. She'd hesitated about leaving one in his letterbox, but had decided that the likelihood of the Chairman being bothered with such ephemera was nil. 'Thanks.'

'Nothing to do with me,' he said. 'That's the office manager's responsibility. But one of the receptionists was raving about a garden design course she'd been on.'

'Well, great.' There it was, that problem with her breathing again. 'It is very popular, although they're all pretty solidly booked. I've got a full house at the moment for a two-day Christmas workshop.'

Best to put off telling Robbie the bad news until after tea, when they'd all gone home, she thought. They wouldn't be able to talk until then, anyway.

'You don't sound particularly happy about that,' Adam said. 'Being booked solid.'

'No.' She shrugged. Then, aware that he was looking at her, waiting for an explanation, 'I'm going to have to spend the entire weekend on the telephone cancelling next year's programme.'

Letting down all those wonderful lecturers who ran the classes, many of whom had become close friends. Letting down the people who'd booked, many of them regulars who looked forward to a little break away from home in the company of like-minded people.

And then there were the standing orders for her own little 'Coleridge House' cottage industry. The homemade fudge and toffee. The honey.

'Cancel the courses?' Adam was frowning. 'Are you saying that your grandfather didn't leave you the house?'

The breeze was much colder coming off the lake and May really was shivering now.

'Yes. I mean, no…He left it to me, but there are conditions involved.'

Conditions her grandfather had known about but had never thought worth mentioning before the stroke had robbed him of so much of his memory.

But why would he? There had been plenty of time back then. And he'd done a major matchmaking job with Michael Linton, a little older, steady as a rock and looking for a well brought up, old-fashioned girl to run his house, provide him with an heir and a spare or two. The kind of man her mother had been supposed to marry.

'What kind of conditions?' Adam asked.

'Ones that I don't meet,' she said abruptly, as keen to change the subject as he had been a few moments earlier.

The morning had been shocking enough without sharing the humiliating entailment that Freddie Jennings had missed when he'd read her grandfather's

very straightforward will after the funeral. The one
Grandpa had made after her mother died which, after
generous bequests to his favourite charities, bequeathed
everything else he owned to his only living relative, his
then infant granddaughter, Mary Louise Coleridge.

Thankfully, they'd reached the small gate that led
directly from the garden of her family home into the
park and May was able to avoid explanations as,
hanging onto the kitten, she fumbled awkwardly in her
handbag for her key.

But her hands were shaking as the shock of the
morning swept over her and she dropped it. Without a
word, Adam picked it up, unlocked the gate, then,
taking her arm to steady her, he pushed the buggy up
through the garden towards the rear of the house.

She stopped in the mud room and filled a saucer with
milk from the fridge kept for animal food. The kitten
trampled in it, lapping greedily, while she lined a cardboard box with an old fleece she used for gardening.

Only when she'd tucked it up safely in the warm was
she able to focus on her own mess.

Her jacket had an ominous wet patch and her skirt
was plastered with mud. It was her best black suit and
maybe the dry cleaners could do something with it,
although right at the moment she didn't want to see it
ever again.

As she unzipped the skirt, let it drop to the floor and
kicked it in the corner, Adam cleared his throat, reminding her that he was there. As if every cell in her
body wasn't vibrating with the knowledge.

'Robbie will kill me if I track dirt through the house,'
she said, peeling off the shredded tights and running a
towel under the tap to rub the mud off her feet. Then,

as he kicked off his mud spattered shoes and slipped the buckle on his belt, 'What are you doing?'

'I've been on the wrong side of Hatty Robson,' he replied. 'If she's coming at me with antiseptic, I want her in a good mood.'

May swallowed hard and, keeping her eyes firmly focused on Nancie, followed him into the warmth of the kitchen with the buggy, leaving him to hang his folded trousers over the Aga, only looking up at a burst of laughter from the garden.

It was the Christmas Workshop crossing the court-yard, heading towards the house for their mid-morning break.

'Flapjacks!'

'What?'

She turned and blinked at the sight of Adam in his shirt tails and socks. 'We're about to have company,' she said, unscrambling her brain and, grabbing the first aid box from beneath the sink, she said, 'Come on!' She didn't stop to see if he was following, but beat a hasty retreat through the inner hall and up the back stairs. 'Bring Nancie!'

Adam, who had picked up the buggy, baby, bag and all to follow, found he had to take a moment to catch his breath when he reached the top.

'Are you all right?' she asked.

'The buggy is heavier than it looks. Do you want to tell me what that was all about?'

'While the appearance of Adam Wavell, minus trousers, in my kitchen would undoubtedly have been the highlight of the week for my Christmas Workshop ladies...' and done her reputation a power of good '...I could not absolutely guarantee their discretion.'

'The highlight?' he asked, kinking up his eyebrow in a well-remembered arc.

'The most excitement I can usually offer is a new cookie recipe. While it's unlikely any of them will call the news desk at *Celebrity*, you can be sure they'd tell all their friends,' she said, 'and sooner or later someone would be bound to realise that you plus a baby makes it a story with the potential to earn them a bob or two.' Which wiped the suspicion of a grin from his face.

'So what do we do now?' he asked. 'Hide at the top of the stairs until they've gone?'

'No need for that,' she said, opening a door that revealed a wide L-shaped landing. 'Come on, I'll clean up your hand while you pray to high heaven that Nancie doesn't wake up and cry.'

Nancie, right on cue, opened incredibly dark eyes and, even before she gave a little whimper, was immediately the centre of attention.

May shoved the first aid box into Adam's hand.

'Shh-sh-shush, little one,' she said as she lifted her out of the buggy, leaving Adam to follow her to the room that had once been her nursery.

When she'd got too old for a nanny, she'd moved into the empty nanny's suite, which had its own bathroom and tiny kitchenette, and had turned the nursery into what she'd been careful to describe as a sitting room rather than a study, using a table rather than a desk for her school projects.

Her grandfather had discouraged her from thinking about university—going off and 'getting her head filled with a lot of nonsense' was what he'd actually said. Not that it had been a possibility once she'd dropped out of school even if she'd wanted to. She hadn't been blessed with her mother's brain and school had been bad enough. Why would anyone voluntarily lengthen the misery?

When she'd begun to take over the running of the house, she'd used her grandmother's elegant little desk in her sitting room, but her business needed a proper office and she'd since converted one of the old pantries, keeping this room as a place of refuge for when the house was filled with guests. When she needed to be on her own.

'Shut the door,' she said as Adam followed her in with the buggy. 'Once they're in the conservatory talking ten to the dozen over a cup of coffee, they won't hear Nancie even if she screams her head off.'

For the moment the baby was nuzzling contently at her shoulder, although, even with her minimal experience, she suspected that wasn't a situation that would last for long.

'The bathroom's through there. Wash off the mud and I'll do the necessary with the antiseptic wipes so that you can get on your way.'

'What about you?'

'I can wait.'

'No, you can't. Heaven knows what's lurking in that mud,' he replied as, without so much as a by-your-leave, he took her free hand, led her through her bedroom and, after a glance around to gain his bearings, into the bathroom beyond. 'Are your tetanus shots up to date?' he asked, quashing any thought that his mind was on anything other than the practical.

'Yes.' She was the most organised woman in the entire world when it came to the details. It was a family trait. One more reason to believe that her grandfather hadn't simply let things slide. That he'd made a deliberate choice to keep things as they were.

Had her mother known about the will? she wondered.

Been threatened with it?

'Are yours?' she asked.

'I imagine so. I pay good money for a PA to deal with stuff like that,' he said, running the taps, testing the water beneath his fingers.

'Efficient, is she?' May asked, imagining a tall, glamorous female in a designer suit and four-inch heels.

'He. Is that too hot?'

She tested it with her fingertips. 'No, it's fine,' she said, reaching for the soap. 'Is that common? A male PA?'

'I run an equal opportunities company. Jake was the best applicant for the job and yes, he is frighteningly efficient. I'm going to have to promote him to executive assistant if I want to keep him. Hold on,' he said. 'You can't do that one-handed.'

She had anticipated him taking Nancie from her, but instead he unfastened his cuffs, rolled back his sleeves and, while she was still transfixed by his powerful wrists, he took the soap from her.

'No!' she said as she realised what he was about to do. He'd already worked the soap into a lather, however, and, hampered by the baby, she could do nothing as he stood behind her with his arms around her, took her scratched hand in his and began to wash it with extreme thoroughness. Finger by finger. Working his thumb gently across her palm where she'd grazed it when she'd fallen. Over her knuckles. Circling her wrist.

'The last time anyone did this, I was no more than six years old,' she protested in an attempt to keep herself from being seduced by the sensuous touch of long fingers, silky lather. The warmth of his body as he leaned into her back, his chin against her shoulder. His cheek against hers. The sensation of being not quite in control of any part of her body whenever he was within touching distance, her heartbeat amplified so that he, and everyone within twenty yards, must surely hear.

'Six?' he repeated, apparently oblivious to her confusion. 'What happened? Did you fall off your pony?'

'My bike. I never had a pony.' She'd scraped her knee and had her face pressed against Robbie's apron. She'd been baking and the kitchen had been filled with the scent of cinnamon, apples, pastry cooking as she'd cleaned her up, comforted her.

Today, it was the cool, slightly rough touch of Adam's chin against her cheek but there was nothing safe or comforting about him. She associated him with leather, rain, her heartbeat raised with fear, excitement, a pitiful joy followed by excruciating embarrassment. Despair at the hopelessness of her dreams.

There had been no rain today, there was no leather, but the mingled scents of clean skin, warm linen, shampoo were uncompromisingly male and the intimacy of his touch was sending tiny shock waves through her body, disturbing her in ways unknown to that green and heartbroken teen.

Oblivious to the effect he was having on her, he took an antiseptic wipe from the first aid box and finished the job.

'That's better. Now let's take a look at your arm.'

'My arm?'

'There's blood on your sleeve.'

'Is there?' While she was craning to see the mingled mud and watery red mess that was never going to wash out whatever the detergent ads said, he had her shirt undone. No shaky-fingered fumbling with buttons this time. She was still trying to get her tongue, lips, teeth into line to protest when he eased it off her shoulder and down her arm with what could only be described as practised ease.

'Ouch. That looks painful.'

She was standing in nothing but her bra and pants and he was looking at her elbow? Okay, her underwear might be lacy but it was at the practical, hold 'em up, rather than push 'em up end of the market. But, even if she wasn't wearing the black lace, scarlet woman underwear, the kind of bra that stopped traffic and would make Adam Wavell's firm jaw drop, he could at least *notice* that she was practically naked.

In her dreams… Her nightmares…

His jaw was totally under control as he gave his full attention to her elbow.

'This might sting a bit…'

It should have stung, maybe it did, but she was feeling no pain as his thick dark hair slid over his forehead, every perfectly cut strand moving in sleek formation as he bent to work. Only a heat that began low her belly and spread like a slow fuse along her thighs, filling her breasts, her womb with an aching, painful need that brought a tiny moan to her lips.

'Does that hurt?' he asked, looking up, grey eyes creased in concern. 'Maybe you should go to Casualty, have an X-ray just to be on the safe side.'

'No,' she said quickly. 'It's fine. Really.'

It was a lie. It wasn't fine; it was humiliating, appalling to respond so mindlessly to a man who, when he saw you in public, put the maximum possible distance between you. To want him to stop looking at her scabby elbow and look at her. See her. Want her.

As if.

These days he was never short of some totally gorgeous girl to keep him warm at night. The kind who wore 'result' shoes and bad girl underwear.

She was more your wellington boots kind of woman. Good skin and teeth, reasonable if boringly brown eyes, but that was it. There was nothing about her that would catch the eye of a man who, these days, had everything.

'You're going to have a whopping bruise,' he said, looking up, catching her staring at him.

'I'll live.'

'This time. But maybe you should consider giving up climbing trees,' he said, pulling a towel down from the pile on the rack, taking her hand in his and patting it dry before working his way up her arm.

'I keep telling myself that,' she said. 'But you know how it is. There's some poor creature in trouble and you're the only one around. What can you do?'

'I'll give you my cell number...' He tore open another antiseptic wipe and took it over the graze on her elbow. Used a second one on his own hand. 'Next time,' he said, looking up with a smile that was like a blow in the solar plexus, 'call me.'

Oh, sure...

'I thought you said you were going to South America.'

'No problem. That's what I have a personal assistant for. You call me, I'll call Jake and he'll ride to your rescue.'

In exactly the same way that he was using her to take care of Nancie, she thought.

'Wouldn't it be easier to give me his number? Cut out the middle sidekick.'

'And miss out on having you shout at me?'

First the blow to the solar plexus, then a jab behind the knees and she was going down…

'That's all part of the fun,' he added.

Fun. Oh, right. She was forgetting. She was the clown…

'My legs are muddy. I really need to take a shower,' she added before he took it upon himself to wash them, too. More specifically, she needed to get some clothes on and get a grip. 'There's a kettle in the kitchenette if you want to make yourself a drink before you go.'

She didn't give him a chance to argue, but dumped Nancie in his arms and, closing her ears to the baby's outraged complaint, shut the door on him.

She couldn't lock it. The lock had broken years ago and she hadn't bothered to get it fixed. Why would she when she shared the house with her invalid grandfather and Robbie, neither of whom were ever going to surprise her in the shower?

Nor was Adam, she told herself as, discarding what little remained of her modesty, she dumped her filthy shirt in the wash basket, peeled off her underwear and stepped under the spray.

It should have been a cold shower, something to quench the fizz of heat bubbling through her veins.

Since it was obvious that even when she was ninety Adam Wavell would have the same effect on her, with or without his trousers, she decided to forgo the pain and turned up the temperature.

CHAPTER THREE

ADAM took a long, slow breath as the bathroom door closed behind him.

The rage hadn't dimmed with time, but neither had the desire. Maybe it was all part of the same thing. He hadn't been good enough for her then and, despite his success, she'd never missed an opportunity to make it clear that he never would be.

But she wasn't immune. And, since a broken engagement, there had never been anyone else in her life. She hadn't gone to university, never had a job, missing out on the irresponsible years when most of their contemporaries were obsessed with clothes, clubbing, falling in and out of love.

Instead, she'd stayed at home to run Coleridge House, exactly like some Edwardian miss, marking time until she was plucked off the shelf, at which point she would do pretty much the same thing for her husband. And, exactly like a good Edwardian girl, she'd abandoned a perfect-fit marriage without hesitation to take on the job of caring for her grandfather after his stroke. Old-fashioned. A century out of her time.

According to the receptionist who'd been raving

about the garden design course, what May Coleridge
needed was someone to take her in hand, help her lose
a bit of weight and get a life before she spread into a
prematurely middle-aged spinsterhood, with only her
strays to keep her warm at night.

Clearly his receptionist had never seen her strip off
her skirt and tights or she'd have realised that there
was nothing middle-aged about her thighs, shapely
calves or a pair of the prettiest ankles he'd ever had the
pleasure of following up a flight of stairs.

But then he already knew all that.

Had been the first boy to ever see those lush curves,
the kind that had gone out of fashion half a century ago,
back before the days of Twiggy and the Swinging
Sixties.

But when he'd unbuttoned her shirt—the alternative
had been relieving her of Nancie and he wasn't about
to do that; he'd wanted her to feel the baby clinging to
her, needing her—he'd discovered that his memory had
served him poorly as he was confronted with a cleavage
that required no assistance from either silicon or a well
engineered bra. It was the real thing. Full, firm, ripe, the
genuine peaches and cream experience—the kind of
peaches that would fill a man's hand, skin as smooth
and white as double cream—and his only thought had
been how wrong his receptionist was about May.

She didn't need to lose weight.

Not one gram.

May would happily have stayed under the shower until
the warm water had washed away the entire ghastly
morning. Since that was beyond the power of mere
water, she contented herself with a squirt of lemon-

scented shower gel and a quick sluice down to remove all traces of mud before wrapping herself in a towel.

But while, on the surface, her skin might be warmer, she was still shivering.

Shock would do that, even without the added problem of the Adam Wavell effect.

Breathlessness. A touch of dizziness whenever she saw him. Something she should have grown out of with her puppy fat. But the puppy fat had proved as stubbornly resistant as her pathetic crush on a boy who'd been so far out of her reach that he might as well have been in outer space. To be needed by him had once been the most secret desire shared only with her diary.

Be careful what you wish for, had been one of Robbie's warnings from the time she was a little girl and she'd been right in that, as in everything.

Adam needed her now. 'But only to take care of Saffy's baby,' she muttered, ramming home the point as she towelled herself dry before wrapping herself from head to toe in a towelling robe. She'd exposed enough flesh for one day.

She needn't have worried. Adam had taken Nancie through to the sitting room and closed the door behind him. Clearly he'd seen more than enough of her flesh for one day.

Ignoring the lustrous dark autumn gold cord skirt she'd bought ages ago in a sale and never worn, she pulled on the scruffiest pair of jogging pants and sweatshirt that she owned. There was no point in trying to compete with the girls he dated these days. Lean, glossy thoroughbreds.

She had more in common with a Shetland pony. Small, overweight, a shaggy-maned clown.

What was truly pathetic was that, despite knowing all that, if circumstances had permitted, May knew she would have still succumbed to his smile. Taken care of Saffy's adorable baby, grateful to have the chance to be that close to him, if only for a week or two while her mother was doing what came naturally. Being bad by most people's standards, but actually having a life.

Nancie began to grizzle into his shoulder and Adam instinctively began to move, shushing her as he walked around May's private sitting room, scarcely able to believe it had been so easy to breach the citadel.

He examined the pictures on her walls. Her books. Picked up a small leather-bound volume lying on a small table, as if she liked to keep it close to hand.

Shakespeare's *Sonnets*. As he replaced it, something fluttered from between the pages. A rose petal that had been pressed between them. As he bent to pick it up, it crumbled to red dust between his fingers and for a moment he remembered a bunch of red roses that, in the middle of winter, had cost him a fortune. Every penny of which had to be earned labouring in the market before school.

He moved on to a group of silver-framed photographs. Her grandparents were there. Her mother on the day she'd graduated. He picked up one of May, five or six years old, holding a litter of kittens and, despite the nightmare morning he was having, the memories that being here had brought back into the sharpest focus, he found himself smiling.

She might have turned icy on him but she was still prepared to risk her neck for a kitten. And any pathetic creature in trouble would have got the same response, whether it was a drowning bird on the school roof—and they'd both been given the maximum punishment short of suspension for that little escapade—or a kitten up a tree.

Not that she was such an unlikely champion of the pitiful.

She'd been one of those short, overweight kids who were never going to be one of the cool group in her year at school. And the rest of them had been too afraid of being seen to be sucking up to the girl from the big house to make friends with her.

She really should have been at some expensive private school with her peers instead of being tossed into the melting pot of the local comprehensive. One of those schools where they wore expensive uniforms as if they were designer clothes. Spoke like princesses.

It wasn't as if her family couldn't afford it. But poor little May Coleridge's brilliant mother—having had the benefit of everything her birth could bestow—had turned her back on her class and become a feminist firebrand who'd publicly deplored all such elitism and died of a fever after giving birth in some desperately inadequate hospital in the Third World with no father in evidence.

If her mother had lived, he thought, May might well have launched a counter-rebellion, demanding her right to a privileged education if only to declare her own independence of spirit; but how could she rebel against someone who'd died giving her life?

Like her mother, though, she'd held on to who she was, refusing to give an inch to peer pressure to slur the perfect vowels, drop the crisp consonants, hitch up her skirt and use her school tie as a belt. To seek anonymity in the conformity of the group. Because that would have been a betrayal, too. Of who she was.

It was what had first drawn him to her. His response to being different had been to keep his head down, hoping to avoid trouble and he'd admired, envied her quiet, obstinate courage. Her act first, think later response to any situation.

Pretty much what had got them into so much trouble in the first place.

Nancie, deciding that she required something a little more tangible than a 'sh-shush' and a jiggle, opened her tiny mouth to let out an amazingly loud wail. He replaced the photograph. Called May.

The water had stopped running a while ago and, when there was no reply, he tapped on the bedroom door.

'Help!'

There was no response.

'May?' He opened the door a crack and then, since there wasn't a howl of outrage, he pushed it wide.

The room, a snowy indulgence of pure femininity, had been something of a shock. For some reason he'd imagined that the walls of her bedroom would be plastered in posters of endangered animals. But the only picture was a watercolour of Coleridge House painted when it was still surrounded by acres of parkland. A reminder of who she was?

There should have been a sense of triumph at having made it this far into her inner sanctum. But looking at that picture made him feel like a trespasser.

May pushed open the door to her grandfather's room. She still thought of it as his room even though he'd

long ago moved downstairs to the room she'd converted
for him, determined that he should be as comfortable
as possible. Die with dignity in his own home.

'May?'

She jumped at the sound of Adam's voice.

'Sorry, I didn't mean to startle you, but Nancie is
getting fractious.'

'Maybe she needs changing. Or feeding.' His only
response was a helpless shrug. 'Both happen on a
regular basis, I understand,' she said, turning to the
wardrobe, hunting down one of her grandfather's silk
dressing gowns, holding it out to him. 'You'd better put
this on before you go and fetch your trousers.' Then, as
he took it from her, she realised her mistake. He
couldn't put it on while he was holding the baby.

Nancie came into her arms like a perfect fit. A soft,
warm, gorgeous bundle of cuddle nestling against her
shoulder. A slightly damp bundle of cuddle.

'Changing,' she said.

'Yes,' he said, tying the belt around his waist and
looking more gorgeous than any man wearing a
dressing gown that was too narrow across the shoulders,
too big around the waist and too short by a country mile
had any right to look.

'You knew!'

'It isn't rocket science,' he said, looking around him.
'This was your grandfather's room.'

It wasn't a question and she didn't bother to answer.
She could have, probably should have, used the master
bedroom to increase the numbers for the arts and crafts
weekends she hosted, but hadn't been able to bring
herself to do that. While he was alive, it was his room
and it still looked as if he'd just left it to go for a stroll

in the park before dropping in at the Crown for lunch with old friends.

The centuries-old furniture gleamed. There were fresh sheets on the bed, his favourite Welsh quilt turned back as if ready for him. And a late rose that Robbie had placed on the dressing table glowed in the thin sunshine.

'Impressive.'

'As you said, Adam, he was an impressive man,' she said, turning abruptly and, leaving him to follow or not as he chose, returned to her room.

He followed.

'You're going to have to learn how to do this,' she warned as she fetched a clean towel from her bathroom and handed it to him.

He opened it without a word, lay it over the bed cover and May placed Nancie on it. She immediately began to whimper.

'Watch her,' she said, struggling against the instinct to pick her up again, comfort her. 'I'll get her bag.'

Ignoring his, 'Yes, ma'am,' which was on a par with the ironic 'Mouse', she unhooked Nancie's bag from the buggy, opened it, found a little pink drawstring bag that contained a supply of disposable nappies and held one out to him.

'Me?' He looked at the nappy, the baby and then at her. 'You're not kidding, are you?' She continued to hold out the nappy and he took it without further comment. 'Okay. Talk me through it.'

'What makes you think I know anything about changing a baby? And if you say that I'm a woman, you are on your own.'

Adam, on the point of saying exactly that, reconsidered. He'd thought that getting through the door would be the problem but that had been the easy part. Obviously, he was asking a lot but, considering Saffy's confidence and her own inability to resist something helpless, he was meeting a lot more resistance from May than he'd anticipated.

'You really know nothing about babies?'

'Look around you, Adam. The last baby to occupy this nursery was me.'

'This was your nursery?' he said, taking in the lace-draped bed, the pale blue carpet, the lace and velvet draped window where she'd stood and watched his humiliation at the hands of her 'impressive' grandfather.

'Actually, this was the nanny's room,' she said. 'The nursery was out there.'

'Lucky nanny.' The room, with its bathroom, was almost as big as the flat he'd grown up in.

May saw the casual contempt with which he surveyed the room but didn't bother to explain that her grandfather had had it decorated for her when she was fifteen. That it reflected the romantic teenager she'd been rather than the down-to-earth woman she'd become.

'As I was saying,' she said, doing her best to hold onto reality, ignore the fact that Adam Wavell was standing in her bedroom, 'the last baby to occupy this nursery was me and only children of only children don't have nieces and nephews to practise on.' Then, having given him a moment for the reality of her ignorance to sink in, she said, 'I believe you have to start with the poppers of her sleep suit.'

'Right,' he said, looking at the nappy, then at the infant and she could almost see the cogs in his brain turning as he decided on a change of plan. That his best move would be to demonstrate his incompetence and wait for her to take over.

He set about unfastening the poppers but Nancie, thinking it was a game, kicked and wriggled and flung her legs up in the air. Maybe she'd maligned him. Instead of getting flustered, he laughed, as if suddenly realising that she wasn't just an annoying encumbrance but a tiny person.

'Come on, Nancie,' he begged. 'I'm a man. This is new to me. Give me a break.'

Maybe it was the sound of his voice, but she lay still, watching him with her big dark eyes, her little forehead furrowed in concentration as if she was trying to work out who he was.

And, while his hands seemed far too big for the delicate task of removing the little pink sleep suit, if it had been his intention to look clumsy and incompetent, he was failing miserably.

The poppers were dealt with, the nappy removed in moments and his reward was a great big smile.

'Thanks, gorgeous,' he said softly. And then leaned down and kissed her dark curls.

The baby grabbed a handful of his hair and, as she watched the two of them looking at one another, May saw the exact moment when Adam Wavell fell in love with his baby niece. Saw how he'd be with his own child.

Swallowing down a lump the size of her fist, she said, 'I'll take that, shall I?' And, relieving him of the nappy, she used it as an excuse to retreat to the bathroom to dispose of it in the pedal bin. Taking her time over washing her hands.

'Do I need to use cream or powder or something?' he called after her.

'I've no idea,' she said, gripping the edge of the basin.

'Babies should come with a handbook. Have you got a computer up here?'

'A what?'

'I could look it up on the web.'

'Oh, for goodness' sake!' She abandoned the safety of the bathroom and joined him beside the bed. 'She's perfectly dry,' she said, after running her palm over the softest little bottom imaginable. 'Just put on the nappy and…and get yourself a nanny, Adam.'

'Easier said than done.'

'It's not difficult. I can give you the number of a reliable agency.'

'Really? And why would you have their number?'

'The Garland Agency provide domestic and nursing staff, too. I needed help. The last few months…'

'I'm sorry. I didn't think.' He turned away, opened the nappy, examined it to see how it worked. 'However, there are a couple of problems with the nanny scenario. My apartment is an open-plan loft. There's nowhere to put either a baby or a nanny.'

'What's the other problem?' He was concentrating on fastening the nappy and didn't answer. 'You said there were a couple of things.' He shook his head and, suddenly suspicious, she said, 'When was the last time you actually saw Saffy?'

'I've been busy,' he said, finally straightening. 'And she's been evasive,' he added. 'I bought a lease on a flat for her in Paris, but I've just learned that she's moved out, presumably to move in with Nancie's father. She's sublet it and has been pocketing the rent for months.'

'You're not a regular visitor, then?'

'You know what she's like, May. I didn't even know she was pregnant.'

'And the baby's father? Who is he?'

'His name is Michel. That's all I know.'

'Poor Saffy,' she said. And there was no doubt that she was pitying her her family.

'She could have come to me,' he protested. 'Picked up the phone.'

'And you'd have done what? Sent her a cheque?'

'It's what she usually wants. You don't think she ever calls to find out how I am, do you?'

'You are strong. She isn't. How was she when she left the baby with you?'

'I'd better wash my hands,' he said.

Without thinking, she put out her hand and grabbed his arm to stop him. 'What aren't you telling me, Adam?'

He didn't answer, but took a folded sheet of paper from his shirt pocket and gave it to her before retreating to the bathroom.

It looked as if it had been screwed up and tossed into a bin, then rescued as an afterthought.

She smoothed it out. Read it.

'Saffy's on the run from her baby's father?' she asked, looking up as he returned. 'Where did she leave the baby?'

'In my office. I found her there when I left a meeting to fetch some papers. Saffy had managed to slip in and out without anyone seeing her. She hasn't lost the skills she learned as a juvenile shoplifter.'

'She must have been absolutely desperate.'

'Maybe she is,' he said. 'But not nearly as desperate as I am right at this minute. I know you haven't got the time of day for me, but she said you'd help her.'

'I would,' she protested. 'Of course I would…'

'But?'

'Where's your mother?' she asked.

'She relocated to Spain after my father died.'

'Moving everyone out of town, Adam? Out of sight, out of mind?'

A tightening around his mouth suggested that her barb had found its mark. And it was unfair. He'd turned his life around, risen above the nightmare of his family. Saffy hadn't had his strength, but she still deserved better from him than a remittance life in a foreign country. All the bad things she'd done had been a cry for the attention, love she craved.

'She won't have gone far.'

'That's not the impression she gives in her note.'

'She'll want to know the baby is safe.' Then, turning on him, 'What about you?'

'Me?'

'Who else?' she demanded fiercely because Adam was too close, because her arms were aching to pick up his precious niece. She busied herself instead, fastening Nancie into her suit. 'Can't you take paternity leave or something?'

'I'm not the baby's father.'

'Time off, then. You do take holidays?'

'When I can't avoid it.' He shook his head. 'I told you. I'm leaving for South America tomorrow.'

'Can't you put it off?'

'It's not just a commercial trip, May. There are politics involved. Government agencies. I'm signing fair trade contracts with cooperatives. I've got a meeting with the President of Samindera that it's taken months to set up.'

'So the answer is no.'

'The answer is no. It's you,' he said, 'or I'm in trouble.'

'In that case you're in trouble.' She picked up the baby and handed her to him, as clear a statement as she could make. 'I'd help Saffy in a heartbeat if I could but—'

'But you wouldn't cross the road to help me.'

'No!'

'Just cross the road to avoid speaking to me. Would I have got anywhere at all if you hadn't been stuck up a tree? Unable to escape?'

That was so unfair! He had no idea. No clue about all the things she'd done for him and it was on the tip of her tongue to say so.

'I'm sorry. You must think I've got some kind of nerve even asking you.'

'No… Of course I'd help you if I could. But I've got a few problems of my own.'

'Tell me,' he said, lifting his spare hand to wipe away the stupid tear that had leaked despite her determination not to break down, not to cry, his fingers cool against her hot cheek. 'Tell me about the world of trouble you're in.'

'I didn't think you'd heard.'

'I heard but you asked where Saffy was…' He shook his head. 'I'm sorry, May, I've been banging on about my own problems instead of listening to yours.' His hand opened to curve gently around her cheek. 'It was something about the house. Tell me. Maybe I can help.'

She shook her head, struggling with the temptation to lean into his touch, to throw herself into his arms, spill out the whole sorry story. But there was no easy comfort.

All she had left was her dignity and she tore herself away, took a step back, then turned away to look out of the window.

'Not this time, Adam,' she said, her voice as crisp as new snow. 'This isn't anything as simple as getting stuck up a tree. The workshop ladies have returned to the stables. It's safe for you to leave now.'

She'd been sure that would be enough to drive him away, but he'd followed her. She could feel the warmth of his body at her shoulder.

'I'm pretty good at complicated, too,' he said, his voice as gentle as the caress of his breath against her hair.

'From what I've read, you've had a lot of practice,' she said, digging her nails into her hands. 'I'm sure you mean well, Adam, but there's nothing you can do.'

'Try me,' he challenged.

'Okay.' She swung around to face him. 'If you've got a job going for someone who can provide food and accommodation for a dozen or so people on a regular basis, run a production line for homemade toffee, is a dab hand with hospital corners, can milk a goat, keep bees and knows how to tame a temperamental lawnmower, that would be a start,' she said in a rush.

'You need a job?' Adam replied, brows kinked up in a confident smile. As if he could make the world right for her by lunch time and still have time to add another company or two to his portfolio. 'Nothing could be simpler. I need a baby minder. I'll pay top rates if you can start right now.'

'The one job for which I have no experience, no qualifications,' she replied. 'And, more to the point, no licence.'

'Licence?'

'I'm not related to Nancie. Without a child-minding licence, it would be illegal.'

'Who would know?' he asked, without missing a beat.

'You're suggesting I don't declare the income to the taxman? Or that the presence of a baby would go unnoticed?' She shook her head. 'People are in and out of here all the time and it would be around the coffee morning circuit faster than greased lightning. Someone from Social Services would be on the doorstep before I could say "knife".' She shrugged. 'Of course, most of the old tabbies would assume Nancie was mine. "*Just like her mother…*"' she said, using the disapproving tone she'd heard a hundred times. Although, until now, not in reference to her own behaviour.

'You're right,' he said, conceding without another word. 'Obviously your reputation is far too precious a commodity to be put at risk.'

'I didn't say that,' she protested.

'Forget it, May. I should have known better.' He shrugged. 'Actually, I did know better but I thought you and Saffy had some kind of a bond. But it doesn't matter. I'll call the authorities. I have no doubt that Nancie's father has reported her missing by now and it's probably for the best to leave it to the court to—'

'You can't do that!' she protested. 'Saffy is relying on you to get her out of this mess.'

'Is she? Read her letter again, May.'

CHAPTER FOUR

THERE was the longest pause while he allowed that to sink in. Then he said, 'Is there any chance of that coffee you promised me?'

May started. 'What? Oh, yes, I'm sorry. It's instant; will that do?'

'Anything.'

The tiny kitchenette was in little more than a cupboard, but she had everything to hand and in a few minutes she returned with a couple of mugs.

'I'll get a blanket and you can put Nancie on the floor.'

'Can you do that?'

She didn't answer, just fetched a blanket from the linen cupboard, pausing on the landing to listen. The silence confirmed that the workshop coffee break was over but the thought of going downstairs, facing Robbie with her unlikely visitor, was too daunting.

Back in her sitting room, she laid the folded blanket on the floor, took Nancie from Adam and put her down on it. Then she went and fetched the teddy she'd spotted in her bag. Putting off for as long as possible the moment when she would have to tell Adam the truth.

'I know you just think I'm trying to get you to take this on, dig me out of a hole,' Adam said when she finally returned. Picking up her coffee, clutching it in front of her like a shield, she sat beside him on the sofa. 'But you really are a natural.'

'I think you're just trying to avoid putting off telling me the whole truth.'

'All I know is what's in Saffy's letter.' He dragged long fingers through his dark hair, looking for once less than the assured man, but more like the boy she remembered. 'I've called some of her friends but if she's confided in them, then aren't telling.'

'What about her agent?' she prompted.

'It seems that they parted company months ago. Her modelling career was yet another fantasy, it seems.'

May picked up the letter and read it again. 'She doesn't sound exactly rational. She could be suffering from post-natal depression. Or maybe having Nancie has triggered a bipolar episode. She always did swing between highs and lows.'

'And if she was? Would you help then?' He shook his head before she could answer. 'I'm sorry. That was unfair, but what I need right now, May, is someone I can trust. Someone who knows her. Who won't judge. Or run to the press with this.'

'The press?'

'Something like this would damage me.'

'You! Is that all you're worried about?' she demanded, absolutely furious with him. 'Yourself. Not Saffy? Not Nancie?'

Nancie, startled, threw out a hand, lost her teddy and began to cry. Glad of the chance to put some distance between them, May scrambled to her knees to rescue the toy, give it back to the baby. Stayed with her on the floor to play with her.

'The Garland Agency has a branch in Melchester,' she said. 'I suggest you call them. They've a world class reputation and I have no doubt that discretion comes with the price tag.'

'As I said. There are a number of problems with that scenario. Apart from the fact that my apartment is completely unsuitable. You've read Saffy's letter. They'll want details. They'll want to know where her mother is. Who she is. What right I have to make childcare arrangements. Saffy is on the run, May. There's a court order in place.'

'You must have some idea where she'd go? Isn't there a friend?'

'If anyone else had asked me that I'd have said that if she was in trouble, she'd come to you.' He stared into the cup he was holding. 'I did ring her a few months ago when there was a rumour in one of the gossip mags about her health. Probably someone heard her throwing up and was quick to suggest an eating disorder. But she was bright, bubbly, rushing off to a shoot. At least that's what she said.' He shrugged. 'She was too eager to get me off the phone. And maybe I was too eager to be reassured. I should have known better.'

'She sounds almost frightened.'

'I know. I'm making discreet enquiries, but until I know who this man is I'm not going to hand over my niece. And I'm doing my best to find Saffy, too. But the last thing we need is a hue and cry.'

He put down the mug, knelt beside her.

'This time I'm the one up the drainpipe, Mouse, and it's raining a monsoon. Won't you climb up and rescue me?'

'I wish I could help—'

'There is no one else,' he said, cutting her off.

The unspoken, *And you owe me...* lay unsaid between them. But she knew that, like her, he was remembering the hideous scene when he'd come to the back door, white-faced, clutching his roses. It had remained closed to his knock but he hadn't gone away. He'd stayed there, mulishly stubborn, for so long that her grandfather had chased him away with the hose.

It had been the week before Christmas and the water was freezing but, while he'd been driven from the doorstep, he'd stayed in the garden defiantly, silently staring up at her room, visibly shivering, until it was quite dark.

She'd stood in this window and watched him, unable to do or say anything without making it much, much worse. Torn between her grandfather and the boy she loved. She would have defied her grandpa, just as her mother had defied him, but there had been Saffy. And Adam. And she'd kept the promise that had been wrung from her even though her heart was breaking.

She didn't owe him a thing. She'd paid and paid and paid...

'I can't,' she said, getting up, putting distance between them. 'I told you, I know no more than you do about looking after a baby.'

'I think we both know that your experience as a rescuer of lame ducks puts you streets ahead of me.'

'Nancie is not a duck,' she said a touch desperately. Why wouldn't he just take no for an answer? There must a dozen women who'd fall over themselves to help him out. Why pick on her? 'And, even if she were,' she added, 'I still couldn't help.'

She couldn't help anyone. That was another problem she was going to have to face. Finding homes for her family of strays.

There wasn't much call for a three-legged cat or a blind duck. And then there were the chickens, Jack and Dolly, the bees. She very much doubted if the Crown would consider a donkey and a superannuated nanny goat an asset to the nation's coffers.

'Why not, May?' he insisted. He got to his feet too, but he'd kept his distance. She didn't have to turn to know that his brows would be drawn down in that slightly perplexed look that was so familiar. 'Tell me. Maybe I can help.'

'Trust me,' she said. Nancie had caught hold of her finger and she lifted the little hand to her lips, kissed it. 'You can't help me. No one can.'

Then, since it was obvious that, unless she explained the situation, Adam wasn't going to give up, she told him why.

Why she couldn't help him or Saffy.

Why he couldn't help her.

For a moment he didn't say anything and she knew he would be repeating her words over in his head, exactly as she had done this morning when Freddie had apologetically explained the situation in words of one syllable.

Adam had assumed financial worries to be the problem. Inheritance tax. Despite the downturn in the market, the house was worth a great deal of money and it was going to take a lot of cash to keep the Inland Revenue happy.

'You have to be married by the end of the month or you'll lose the house?' he repeated, just to be certain that he'd understood.

She swallowed, nodded.

She would never have told him if he hadn't been so persistent, he realised. She'd told him that she couldn't help but, instead of asking her why, something he would have done if it had been a work-related problem, he'd been so tied up with his immediate problem that he hadn't been listening.

He was listening now. And there was only one thought in his head. That fate had dropped her into his lap. That the boy who hadn't been good enough to touch Coleridge flesh, who'd shivered as he'd waited for her to defy her grandfather, prove that her hot kisses had been true, now held her future in the palm of his hand.

That he would crack the ice in May Coleridge's body between the fine linen sheets of her grandfather's four-poster bed and listen to the old man spin in his grave as did it.

'What's so important about the end of the month?' he asked. Quietly, calmly. He'd learned not to show his thoughts, or his feelings.

'My birthday. It's on the second of December.'

She'd kept her back to him while she'd told him her problems, but now she turned and looked up at him. She'd looked up at him before, her huge amber eyes making him burn, her soft lips quivering with uncertainty. The taste of them still haunted him.

He'd liked her. Really liked her. She had guts, grit and, despite the wide gulf in their lives, they had a lot in common. And he'd loved being in the quiet, ordered peace of the lovely gardens of Coleridge House, the stables where she'd kept her animals. Everything so clean and well organised.

He'd loved the fact that she had her own kettle to make coffee. That there was always homemade cake in a tin. The shared secrecy. That no one but she knew he was there. Not her grandfather, not his family. It had all been so different from the nightmare of his home life.

But taking her injured animals, helping her look after them was one thing. She wasn't the kind of girl any guy—even one with no pretensions to street cred— wanted to be seen with at the school disco.

But their meetings weren't as secret as he'd thought. His sister had got curious, followed him and black-mailed him into asking May to go as his date to the school disco.

It had been as bad as he could have imagined. While all the other girls had been wearing boob tubes and skirts that barely covered their backsides, she'd been wearing something embarrassingly sedate, scarcely any make-up. He was embarrassed to be seen with her and, ashamed of his embarrassment, had asked her to dance.

That was bad, too. She didn't have a clue and he'd caught hold of her and held her and that had been better. Up close, her hair had smelled like flowers after rain. She felt wonderful, her softness against his thin, hard body had roused him, brought to the surface all those feelings that he'd kept battened down. This was why he'd gone back time after time to the stables. Risked being caught by the gardener. Or, worse, the housekeeper.

Her skin was so beautiful that he'd wanted to touch it, touch her, kiss her. And her eyes, liquid black in the dim lights of the school gym, had told him that she wanted it too. But not there. Not where anyone could see them, hoot with derision…

They had run home through the park. She'd unlocked

the gate, they'd scrambled up to the stables loft and it was hard to say which of them had been trembling the most when he'd kissed her, neither of them doubting what they wanted.

That it was her first kiss was without doubt. It was very nearly his, too. His first real kiss. The taste of her lips, the sweetness, her uncertainty as she'd opened up to him had made him feel like a giant. All powerful. Invincible. And the memory of her melting softness in the darkness jolted through him like an electric charge...

'You need a husband by the end of the month?' he said, dragging himself back from the hot, dark thoughts that were raging through him.

'There's an entailment on Coleridge House,' she said. 'The legatee has to be married by the time he or she is thirty or the house goes to the Crown.'

'He's controlling you, even from the grave,' he said.

She flushed angrily. 'No one knew,' she said.

'No one?'

'My grandfather lost great chunks of his memory when he had the stroke. And papers were lost when Jennings' offices were flooded a few years ago...'

'You're saying you had no warning?'

She shook her head. 'My mother was dead long before she was thirty, but she thought marriage was an outdated patriarchal institution...' The words caught in her throat and she turned abruptly away again so that he shouldn't see the tears turning her caramel-coloured eyes to liquid gold, just as they had that night when her grandfather had dragged her away from him, his coat thrown around her. 'She'd have told them all to go to hell rather than compromise her principles.'

He tried to drown out the crowing triumph. That this

girl, this woman, who from that day to this had crossed the road rather than pass him in the street, was about to lose everything. That her grandfather, that 'impressive' man who thought he was not fit to breathe the same air as his precious granddaughter, had left her at his mercy.

'But before the stroke? He could have told you then.'

'Why would he? I was engaged to Michael, the wedding date was set.'

'Michael Linton.' He didn't need to search his memory. He'd seen the announcement and Saffy had been full of it, torn between envy and disgust.

Envy that May would be Lady Linton with some vast country estate and a house in London. Disgust that she was marrying a man nearly old enough to be her father. 'Her grandfather's arranged it all, of course,' she'd insisted. 'He's desperate to marry her off to someone safe before she turns into her mother and runs off with some nobody who gets her up the duff.' She'd been about to say more but had, for once, thought better of it.

Not that he'd had any argument with her conclusion. But then her grandfather had suffered a massive stroke and the wedding had at first been put off. Then Michael Linton had married someone else.

'What happened? Why didn't you marry him?'

'Michael insisted that Grandpa would be better off in a nursing home. I said no, but he kept bringing me brochures, dragging me off to look at places. He wouldn't listen, wouldn't hear what I was saying, so in the end I gave him his ring back.'

'And he took it?'

'He wanted a wife, a hostess, someone who would fit into his life, run his home. He didn't want to be burdened with an invalid.'

'If he'd taken any notice of your lame duck zoo, he'd have known he was on a hiding to nothing.'

She shook her head and when she looked back over her shoulder at him her eyes were sparkling, her cheeks wet, but her lips were twisted into a smile.

'Michael didn't climb over the park gate when the gardener was looking the other way, Adam. He was a front door visitor.'

'You mean you didn't make him help you muck out the animals?' he asked and was rewarded with a blush.

'I didn't believe he'd appreciate the honour. He'd have been horrified if he'd seen me shin up a tree to save a kitten. Luckily, the situation never arose when he was around.' A tiny shuddering breath escaped her. 'You don't notice creatures in distress from the back seat of a Rolls-Royce.'

'His loss,' he said, his own throat thick as the memories of stolen hours rushed back at him.

'And mine, it would seem.'

'You'd have been utterly miserable married to him.' She shook her head.

'You aren't going to take this lying down, are you?' he asked. 'I can't believe it would stand up in a court of law and the tabloids would have a field day if the government took your home.'

'A lot of people are much worse off than me, Adam. I'm not sure that a campaign to save a fifteen-room house for one spoilt woman and her housekeeper would be a popular cause.'

She had a point. She'd been born to privilege and her plight was not going to garner mass sympathy.

'Is that what Freddie Jennings told you?' he asked. 'I assume you have taken legal advice?'

'Freddie offered to take Counsel's opinion but, since Grandpa had several opportunities to remove the Codicil but chose not to, I don't have much of a case.' She lifted her shoulders in a gesture of utter helplessness. 'It makes no difference. The truth is that there's no cash to spare for legal fees. As it is, I'm going to have to sell a load of stuff to meet the inheritance tax bill. Even if I won, the costs would be so high that I'd have to sell the house to pay them. And if I lost...'

If she lost it would mean financial ruin.

Well, that would offer a certain amount of satisfaction. But nowhere near as much as the alternative that gave him everything he wanted.

'So you're telling me that the only reason you can't take care of Nancie is because you're about to lose the house? If you were married, there would be no problem,' he said. He didn't wait for her answer—it hadn't been a question. 'And your birthday is on the second of December. Well, it's tight, but it's do-able.'

'Do-able?' she repeated, her forehead buckled in a frown. 'What are you talking about?'

'A quick trip to the register office, a simple "I do", you get to keep your house and I'll have somewhere safe for Nancie. As her aunt-in-law, I don't imagine there would be any objection to you taking care of her?'

And he would be able to finally scratch the itch that was May Coleridge while dancing on the grave of the man who'd shamed and humiliated him.

But if he'd imagined that she'd fling her arms around him, proclaim him her saviour, well, nothing had changed there, either.

Her eyes went from blank to blazing, like lightning out of a clear blue sky.

'That's not even remotely funny, Adam. Now, if you don't mind, I've got a house full of guests who'll be expecting lunch in a couple of hours.'

She was wearing shabby sweats but swept by him, head high, shoulders back. Despite her lack of inches, the fact that her puppy fat hadn't melted away but had instead evolved into soft curves, she was every inch the lady.

'Mouse…' he protested, shaken out of his triumph by the fact that, even in extremis, she'd turn him down flat. As if he was still a nobody from the wrong side of the tracks. 'May!'

She was at the door before she stopped, looked back at him.

'I'm serious,' he said, a touch more sharply than he'd intended.

She shook her head. 'It's impossible.'

In other words, he might wear hand stitched suits these days instead of the cheapest market jeans, live in an apartment that had cost telephone numbers, be able to buy and sell the Coleridge estate ten times over, but he could never wash off the stink of where he'd come from. That his sister had been a druggie, his mother was no better than she ought to be and his father had a record as long as his arm.

But times had changed. He wasn't that kid any more. What he wanted, he took. And he wanted this.

'It would be a purely temporary arrangement,' he said. 'A marriage of convenience.'

'Are you saying that you wouldn't expect…?'

She swallowed, colour flooding into her cheeks, and it occurred to him that if Michael Linton's courtship had been choreographed by her grandfather it would have been a formal affair rather than a lust-fuelled romance. The thought sent the blood rushing to a very different part of his anatomy and he was grateful for the full stiff folds of the dressing gown he was wearing.

She cleared her throat. 'Are you saying that you wouldn't expect the full range of wifely duties?'

Not the full range. He wouldn't expect her to cook or clean or keep house for him.

'Just a twenty-four seven nanny,' she continued, regaining her composure, assuming his silence was assent. 'Only with more paperwork, a longer notice period and a serious crimp in your social life?'

'I don't have much time for a social life these days,' he assured her before she could gather herself. 'But there are formal business occasions where I would normally take a guest. Civic functions. But you usually attend those, anyway.'

Nancie, as if aware of the sudden tension, let out a wail and, using the distraction to escape the unexpected heat of May's eyes, he picked her up, put her against his shoulder, turned to look at her.

'Well? What do you say?'

She shook her head, clearly speechless, and the band holding her hair slipped, allowing wisps to escape.

Backlit by the sun, they shone around her face like a butterscotch halo.

'What have you got to lose?' he persisted, determined to impose his will on her. Overwrite the Coleridge name with his own.

'Marriage is a lot easier to get into than it is to get out of,' she protested. Still, despite every advantage, resisting him. 'There has to be an easier solution to baby care than marrying the first woman to cross your path.'

'Not the first,' he replied. 'I passed several women in the park and I can assure you that it never crossed my mind to marry any of them.'

'No?'

He'd managed to coax the suggestion of a smile from her.

'Divorce is easy enough if both parties are in agreement,' he assured her. 'You'll be giving up a year of your freedom in return for your ancestral home. It looks like a good deal to me.'

The smile did not materialise. 'I can see the advantage from my point of view,' she said. 'But what's in it for you? You can't really be that desperate to offload Nancie.'

'Who said anything about "offloading" Nancie?' He allowed himself to sound just a little bit offended by her suggestion that he was doing that. 'On the contrary, I'm doing my best to do what her mother asked. It's not as if I intend to leave you to manage entirely on your own. I have to go away tomorrow, but I'll pull my weight until then.'

'Oh, right. And how do you intend to do that?'

'I'll take the night watch. The master bedroom is made up. I'll pack a bag and move in there today.'

CHAPTER FIVE

'WHAT?'

The word was shocked from her.

May swallowed again, tucked a loose strand of hair behind her ear in a nervous gesture that drew attention to her neck. It was long and smooth. She had the clearest ivory skin coloured only by the fading blush...

'If we get married, people will expect us to live together,' he pointed out. 'You wouldn't want the Crown Commissioners getting the impression that it was just a piece of paper, would you? That you were cheating.'

'But—'

Before she could put her real objection into words, Nancie, bless her heart, began to grizzle.

'What do I do now?' he asked, looking at her helplessly. That, at least, wasn't an act.

'I think the fact that she's chewing your neck is the clue,' she said distractedly.

'She's hungry?'

'Feeding her, like changing her nappy, is something that has to happen at regular intervals. No doubt there's a bottle and some formula in that bag.'

She didn't wait for him to check, but went into her bedroom, fetched the bag and emptied it on the table.

'There's just one carton. I wonder what that means.'

'That we'll probably need more very soon,' he replied, picking up on her unspoken thought that it might offer a clue about how long Saffy intended to stay out of sight. Always assuming she was thinking that rationally.

'Adam!' she protested as she turned the carton over, searching for instructions.

'I'm sorry. I can plan a takeover bid to the last millisecond, but I'm out of my depth here.'

'Then get help.'

'I'm doing my best,' he replied. 'If you'd just cooperate we could both get on with our lives.'

May was struggling to keep up a calm, distant front. She'd been struggling ever since he'd stood beneath the tree in the park. Used that ridiculous name.

Inside, everything was in turmoil. Her heart, her pulse were racing.

'Please, Adam…' Her voice caught in her throat. He couldn't mean it. He was just torturing her… 'Don't…'

He lifted his hand, cradling her cheek to still her protest. His touch was gentle. A warm soothing balm that swept through her, taking the tension out of her joints so that her body swayed towards him.

'It wouldn't be that bad, would it, Mouse?'

Bad? How much worse could it get?

'It seems a little…extreme,' she said, resisting with all her will the yearning need to lean into his palm. Surrender everything, including her honour.

'Losing your home, your business, is extreme,' he insisted. 'Getting married is just a piece of paper.'

Not for her...

'A mutually beneficial contract to be cancelled at the convenience of both parties,' he added. 'Think of Robbie, May. Where will she go if you lose the house?'

'She's got a pension. A sister...'

'Your business,' he persisted.

The bank loan...

'And what about your animals? Who else will take them in? You know that most of them will have to be put down.'

'Don't!' she said, her throat so tight that the words were barely audible.

'Hey,' he said, pulling her into her arms so that the three of them were locked together. 'I'm your trusty sidekick, remember? As always, late on the scene but ready to leap into action when you need a helping hand.'

'This is a bit more than a helping hand.'

'Hand, foot and pretty much everything in between,' he agreed. 'Take your pick.'

He was doing his best to make her laugh, she realised, or maybe cry.

Either would be appropriate under the circumstances. What would her mother have done? Spit in the devil's eye? Or screw the patriarchal system, using it against itself to keep both her house and her freedom?

Stupid question. Heaven knew that she was not her mother. If she'd had her courage she'd be long gone. But all she had was her home. Robbie. The creatures that relied on her. The life she'd managed to make for herself.

As for breaking the promise to her grandfather, her punishment for that was built into the bargain of a barren marriage with a self-destruct date.

'May?' he prompted.

Decision time.

What decision…? There was only ever going to be one answer and, taking a deep breath, her heart beating ten times faster than when she'd climbed that tree, her voice not quite steady, she said, 'You're absolutely sure about this? Last chance.'

'Quite sure,' he replied, his own voice as steady as a rock. No hint of doubt, no suggestion of intestinal collywobbles on his part. 'It's a no-brainer.'

'No…' she said, wondering why, even now, she was hesitating.

'No?'

'I mean yes. You're right. It's a no-brainer.'

'Shall we aim for something a little more decisive?' he suggested. 'Just so that we know exactly where we stand?'

'You're not planning on going down on one knee?' she demanded, appalled.

'Heaven forbid. Just something to seal the bargain,' he said, taking his hand from her back and offering it to her.

'A handshake?' she said, suddenly overcome with the urgent need to laugh as she lifted her own to clasp it. 'Well, why not? Everything else appears to be shaking.'

As his hand tightened around hers, everything stilled. Even Nancie stopped nuzzling and grumbling. All she could hear was her pulse pounding through her ears. All she could see were his eyes. Not the bright silver of the boy she'd known but leaden almost unreadable. A shiver ran through her as he closed the gap between them, kissed her, but then she closed her eyes and all sense of danger evaporated in the heat of his mouth, the taste of him and the cherished bittersweet memory flooded back.

It was different. He was different.

The kiss was assured, certain and yet, beneath it all, she recognised the boy who'd lain with her in the stable loft and kissed her, undressed her, touched her. And for a moment she was no longer the woman who'd subjugated her yearning for love, for a family of her own into caring for her grandfather, creating a business, building some kind of life for herself.

As Adam's lips touched hers, she was that girl again and an aching need opened up before her, a dizzying void that tempted her to plunge headlong into danger, to throw caution to the winds and boldly kiss him back.

'Oh…'

At the sound of Robbie's shocked little exclamation, May stumbled back, heat rushing to her face.

That girl reliving the moment of guilt, embarrassment, pain when they'd been discovered…

'Robbie…'

'I thought I heard you come in earlier,' she said.

'I had a fall. In the park. Adam came to my rescue.'

'That would account for the kitten, then,' she said stiffly. 'And the trousers hanging over the Aga.'

'We both got rather muddy,' Adam said.

'I'm sure it's nothing to do with me what you were doing in the park,' Robbie said, ignoring him. 'But Jeremy is here.'

'Jeremy?' she repeated, struggling to gather her wits.

'He's brought the designs for the honey labels.'

'Has he? Oh, right…' Expanding honey production had been part of the future she'd planned and Jeremy Davidson had volunteered to design the labels for her.

'He's doing you a favour, May. You won't want to keep him waiting,' she said primly before turning to leave.

'Robbie, wait!' she began, then glanced at Adam, suddenly unsure of herself. She wanted to tell Robbie that the kiss had meant nothing. That it was no more than a handshake on a deal. Except when Robbie paused, her shoulders stiff with disapproval, the words wouldn't come.

'Go and see the man about your labels,' Adam urged, then nodded, as if to reassure her that she could go ahead with her plans. That she had a future. 'Leave this to me.'

'But Nancie…' She looked at the baby. It was easier than meeting his eyes, looking at Robbie.

'I'll bring her down in a moment.'

Adam watched as she stumbled from the room in her haste to escape her embarrassment and he could have kicked himself.

Most women in her situation would have leapt at the deal he'd offered, no questions asked, but her first response had been flat refusal, anger at his presumption, and that had caught him on the raw.

His kiss had been intended as a marker. A promise to himself that she would pay for every slight, every insult but, instead of the anticipated resistance, she had responded with a heat that had robbed him of any sense of victory. Only left him wanting more.

He did not want her.

He could have any woman he wanted. Beautiful women. The kind who turned heads in the street.

All he wanted from May Coleridge was her pride at his feet. And he would have it.

She had been his last mistake. His only weakness. Since the day he'd walked away from this house, his clothes freezing on his back, he'd never let anything, any emotion, stand in his way.

With his degree in his pocket, a mountain of debt to pay off, his mother incapable of looking after either herself or Saffy, the only job he had been able to get in his home town was in an old import company that had been chugging along happily since the days when the clipper ships brought tea from China. It wasn't what he'd dreamed of, but within five years he'd been running the company. Now he was the chairman of an international company trading commodities from across the globe.

His success didn't appear to impress May's disapproving housekeeper.

'It's been a while, Mrs Robson.'

'It has. But nothing appears to have changed, Mr Wavell,' she returned, ice-cool.

'On the contrary. I'd like you to be the first to know that May and I are going to be married.'

'Married!' And, just like that, all the starch went out of her. 'When…?'

'Before the end of the month.'

'I meant…' She shook her head. 'What's the hurry? What are you after? If you think May's been left well off—'

'I don't need her money. But May needs me. She's just been told that if she isn't married by her birthday, she's going to lose her home.'

'But that's less than four weeks…' She rallied. 'Is that what Freddie Jennings called about in such a flap this morning?'

'I imagine so. Apparently, some ancient entailment turned up when he took James Coleridge's will to probate.'

The colour left her face but she didn't back down. 'Why would you step in to help, Adam Wavell? What do you get out of it?' She didn't give him a chance to answer. 'And that little girl's mother? What will she have to say about it?'

'Nancie,' he said, discovering that a baby made a very useful prop, 'meet Hatty Robson. Mrs Robson, meet my niece.'

'She's Saffy's daughter?' She came closer, the rigid lines of her face softening and she touched the baby's curled up fist. 'She's a pretty thing.' Then, 'So where is your sister? In rehab? In jail?'

'Neither,' he said, hanging onto his temper by a thread. 'But we are having a bit of a family crisis.'

'Nothing new there, then.'

'No,' he admitted. A little humility wouldn't hurt. 'Saffy was sure that May would help.'

'Again? Hasn't she suffered enough for your family?' Suffered?

'I met her in the park. She was up a tree,' he added. 'Rescuing a kitten.'

She rolled her eyes. An improvement.

'The only reason she told me her troubles was to explain why she couldn't look after Nancie.'

'And you leapt in with an immediate marriage proposal. Saving not one, but two women with a single bound?' Her tone, deeply ironic, suggested that, unlike May, she wasn't convinced that it was an act of selfless altruism.

'Make that three,' he replied, raising her irony and calling her. 'I imagine one of May's concerns was you, Mrs Robson. This is your home, too.'

If it hadn't been so unlikely, he would have sworn

she blushed. 'Did she say that?' she demanded, instantly on the defensive. 'I don't matter.'

'You know that's not true,' he said, pushing his advantage. 'You and this house are all she has.'

And this time the blush was unmistakable. 'That's true. Poor child. Well, I'm sure that's very generous of you, Mr Wavell. Just tell me one thing. Why didn't your sister, or you, just pick up the phone and call one of those agencies which supplies temporary nannies? I understand you can afford it these days.'

He'd already explained his reasons to May and he wasn't about to go through them again. 'Just be glad for May's sake,' he replied, 'that I didn't.'

She wasn't happy, clearly didn't trust his motives, but after a moment she nodded just once. 'Very well. But bear this in mind. If you hurt her, you'll have to answer to me. And I won't stop at a hosing down.'

'Hurt her? Why would I hurt her?'

'You've done it before,' she said. 'It's in your nature. I've seen the string of women you've paraded through the pages of the gossip magazines. How many of them have been left with a bruised heart?' She didn't wait for an answer. 'May has spent the last ten years nursing her grandpa. She's grieving for him, vulnerable.'

'And without my help she'll lose her home, her business and the animals she loves,' he reminded her.

She gave him a long look, then said, 'That child is hungry. You'd better give her to me before she chews a hole in your neck. What did you say her name was?'

'Nancie, Mrs Robson. With an i and an e.'

'Well, that's a sweet old-fashioned name,' she said, taking the baby. 'Hello, Nancie.' Then, looking from the baby to him, 'I suppose you'd better call me Robbie.'

'Thank you. Is there anything I can do, Robbie?'

'Go and book a date with the Registrar?' she suggested. 'Although you might want to put your trousers on first.'

The kitchen was empty, apart from a couple of cats curled up on an old armchair and an old mongrel dog who was sharing his basket with a duck and a chicken.

None of them took any notice of him as he unhooked his trousers from the rail above the Aga and carried them through to the mud room, where the kitten had curled up in the fleece and gone to sleep. He hoped Nancie, jerked out of familiar surroundings, her routine, would settle as easily.

Having brushed off the mud as best he could and made himself fit to be seen in polite society, he hunted down May. He found her in a tiny office converted from one of the pantries, shoulder to shoulder with a tall, thin man who was, presumably, Jeremy, as they leaned over her desk examining some artwork.

'May?'

She turned, peering at him over a pair of narrow tortoiseshell spectacles that were perched on the end of her nose. They gave her a cute, kittenish look, he thought. And imagined himself reaching for them, taking them off and kissing her.

'I've talked to Robbie,' he said, catching himself. 'Put her in the picture.'

That blush coloured her cheeks again, but she was back in control of her voice, her breathing as she said, 'You've explained everything?'

'The why, the what and the when,' he assured her. 'I'll give you a call as soon as I've sorted out the details. You'll be in all afternoon?'

'You're going to do it today?' she squeaked. Not that in control…

'It's today, or it's too late.'

'Yes…' Clearly, it was taking some time for the reality of her situation to sink in. 'Will you need me? For the paperwork?'

'I'll find out what the form is and call you. I'll need your number,' he prompted when she didn't respond. 'It's unlisted.'

Flustered, May plucked a leaflet from a shelf above her desk and handed it to him. 'My number is on there.'

For a moment they just looked at one another and he wondered what she was thinking about. The afternoons they'd spent together in the stables with him ducking out of sight whenever anyone had come near? The night when they had been too absorbed in each other to listen? Or the years that had followed…?

'What are you doing?' he asked, turning to look at the artwork laid out on the table.

'What?' He looked up and saw that she was still staring at him and her poise deserted her as, flustered, she said, 'I'm ch-choosing a label for Coleridge House honey. Do you know Jeremy Davidson? He's head of the art department at the High School.' Then, as if she felt she had to explain how she knew him, 'I'm a governor.'

'You're a school governor?' He didn't bother to suppress a grin, and yet why should he be surprised? She'd been born to sit on charitable committees, school boards. In the fullness of time she'd no doubt become a magistrate, like her grandfather. 'I hope you've done something about those overflowing gutters.'

'It was my first concern.' For a moment there was the hint of a smile, the connection of a shared memory, before she turned to Jeremy Davidson. 'Adam and I were at the High School at the same time, Jeremy. He was two years above me.'

'I'm aware that Mr Wavell is one of our more successful ex-pupils,' he said rather stiffly. 'I'm delighted to meet you.'

He was another of those old school tie types. Elegant, educated. A front door visitor who would have met with James Coleridge's approval. His manners were impeccable, even if his smile didn't quite reach his eyes.

'I have an Emma Davidson on my staff,' he said. 'I believe her husband is an art teacher. Is that simply a coincidence or is she your wife?'

'She's my wife,' he admitted.

'I thought she must be. You're on half term break, I imagine. While she's at work catching up with Saminderan employment law, you're here, playing with honey pot labels—'

'*Was* my wife. We're separated.' His glance at May betrayed him. 'Our divorce will be finalised in January.'

'Well, that's regrettable,' he said. 'Emma is a valued member of my organisation.'

'These things happen.'

So they did. But not fast enough to save May, he thought. Were they having an affair? he wondered. Or was she saving herself for the big wedding? Or was he waiting to declare himself until he was free?

Best put him out of his misery. 'Has May told you our good news?' he asked.

'Adam…'

She knew.

'We're getting married later this month,' he continued, as if he hadn't heard her.

Jeremy's shocked expression told its own story and, before he could find the appropriate words, May swiftly intervened.

'I can't decide which design I like best, Adam. What do you think?'

He waited pointedly until Davidson moved out of his way, then put his hand on the desk and leaned forward, blocking him out with his shoulder.

They were pretty enough floral designs with 'Coleridge House Honey' in some fancy script. About right for a stall at a bazaar.

'You produce handmade sweets too, don't you?' he asked her, looking at the shelf and picking up a fairly basic price list that, like the brochure, had obviously been printed on her computer. 'Is this all the literature that you have?'

She nodded as he laid it, with the brochure, beside the labels.

'There's no consistency in design,' he said. 'Not in the colours, or even the fonts you've used. Nothing to make it leap out from the shelf. Coleridge House is a brand, May. You should get some professional help to develop that.'

'Jeremy—'

'There's a rather good watercolour of the house in your bedroom. The country house, nostalgia thing would be a strong image and work well across the board. On labels, price lists and on the front of your workshop brochure.'

She looked up at him, a tiny frown creasing the space between her eyes.

'Just a thought.' With a touch to her shoulder, a curt nod to Davidson, he said, 'I'll call you later.'

He found Robbie in the kitchen preparing a feed for Nancie, who was beginning to sound very cross indeed. Resisting the urge to take the child from her—the whole point of the exercise was to leave Nancie in May's capable hands and not get involved in baby care, or her cottage industry, for that matter—he took a card from his wallet and placed it on the table.

'This is my mobile number should you need to get hold of me urgently.'

'Stick it on the cork board, will you?'

He found a drawing pin and stuck it amongst a load of letters, appointment cards and postcards. The kind of domestic clutter so notably absent from the slate and steel kitchen in his apartment.

'Is this bag all you have?' she asked.

'I'm afraid so. You'll be needing rather more than that, I imagine?'

'You imagine right.'

'Well, just get whatever you want. Better still, make a list and I'll have it delivered. May can give it to me when I ring her about the wedding arrangements.'

Robbie said nothing when May returned to the kitchen after seeing Jeremy Davidson out, just handed her the baby and the feeder and left her to get on with it, while she set about cleaning salad vegetables at the old butler's sink.

'Any hints about how to do this?' she asked, using her toe to hook out a chair so that she could sit down.

'You'll learn the way I did when your grandfather brought you home, no more than a month old,' she said abruptly.

'Robbie…'

'You'll find that if you put it to the little one's mouth she'll do the rest.' She ripped up a head of lettuce. 'Just keep the end of the bottle up so that she's not sucking air.'

May settled the baby in the crook of her arm and, as she offered Nancie the bottle, she latched onto it, sucking greedily. She watched her for a while, then, when Robbie's silence became oppressive, she looked up and said, 'Are you angry with me, Robbie?'

'Angry with you! Why would I be angry with you?'

'You're angry with someone.'

'I'm angry with your grandfather. That foolish, pig-headed old man. Just because your mother wouldn't listen to him. Wouldn't live her life the way he wanted…'

'You're talking about the will?'

'Of course I'm talking about the will. How could he put you in such a position?'

She breathed out a sigh of relief.

She'd been anticipating a tirade about promises made and broken. About marriage being for love, not convenience. She wouldn't take a schoolgirl crush into account.

'The will wasn't about my mother, Robbie,' May said. 'It was about history. Tradition.'

'Tradition, my foot! I can't believe he'd do this to you.'

'He didn't. Not deliberately. He thought I was going to marry Michael. If he'd known…'

'Who knows anything?' she demanded. 'If I'd known my husband was going to drop dead of a heart problem when he was twenty-six I wouldn't have insisted on waiting to have a baby until we had a house, until everything was just as I wanted it…' Without warning, her eyes were full of tears. 'Life is never just as you want it, May. There are no certainties. How could he look after me and not take care of you? It's so cruel,' she said, dashing them away with the back of her hand. 'After the way you cared for him all those years when you could have been married, with a family of your own…'

'Hush, Robbie, it's all right. It's going to be all right,' she repeated, wanting to go to her, comfort her but hampered by Nancie, who had snuggled into her shoulder as if she belonged there.

'Only because Adam Wavell happened by when you needed him.'

'He didn't just happen by. He was on his way to ask for my help. This is a mutual aid package.'

'And if he hadn't needed you? What would you have done then?'

'Well,' she said, 'I was going to sit down and make a list of all the unmarried men I know. Jed Atkins was favourite.'

'Jed!' Robbie snorted. 'Well, he'd be a safer bet than Adam Wavell. And no baby.'

'But hundreds of relations who'd all expect to be invited for Christmas. Would there be a turkey big enough?'

Robbie groaned and they both laughed, but then her smile faded and she said, 'Don't fall for him, May. It's just a piece of paper.'

'I know.'

'Do you?' Robbie asked, her look searching, anxious. 'That kiss…'

'He kissed me to seal the bargain we'd made. It was nothing.'

'Nothing to him.'

'And nothing to me,' she said, pressing her lips tightly together in an attempt to stop them tingling at the memory. Forget the desperate need that his touch had awakened.

Trying not to read too much into his edgy reaction to Jeremy Davidson. The poor man had fallen apart when his wife left him and she'd offered him a distraction with her labels, something to keep his mind occupied. Something to make him feel needed. But the way Adam had made it so obvious that he'd been in her bedroom... If he'd been a dog, she'd have said he was marking his territory.

Which was ridiculous.

Adam only wanted her as a nanny.

'Absolutely nothing,' she said with emphasis. It was only in her head that she'd kissed him back, seduced him with her mouth and then her body...

Robbie made the 'humphing' noise she used when she was unconvinced.

'What did you expect us to do? Shake hands?' she asked, ignoring the fact that it had started out that way.

'Why not? If it's just a business arrangement.'

'We've known one another for a very long time. I see him all the time at civic functions. He's saving my home, for heaven's sake.'

'And you're saving him a world of trouble,' she replied. 'Just remember that as soon as this "family crisis" of his is resolved—'

'He'll be gone.'

'Let's just hope it isn't before he's put the ring on your finger. Signed the register.'

CHAPTER SIX

'He wouldn't…'

'Lead you on, then back out at the last minute? He has no reason to love this family. Be kind to you.'

No reason that he knew.

'He needs my help,' she said. Then, as the baby paused to draw breath, 'Do you think you can manage lunch on your own? I'll have to wash the cot down.'

'Chance would be a fine thing,' she replied, letting it go.

'Sorry?'

'You gave it to the vicar last year. For that family whose house burned down.'

'Oh, fudge! I'd forgotten.'

'Adam said to make a list of anything you need,' Robbie said, resuming her attack on the vegetables.

'Right. I'll do that,' she said, then was distracted by Nancie, who was opening her mouth like a little fish, waving her sweet, plump arms to demand her attention. May was familiar with the powerful instinct to survive in small mammals blindly seeking out their mother's milk, but this urgency in a small helpless baby went straight to her heart.

'An extra pair of hands wouldn't go amiss, either,' Robbie said. 'You've got that order for toffee to deliver by the end of the week.'

'No problem. Adam wants to help. I'll have to clear a wardrobe in Grandpa's room for him.'

'He's moving in? To your grandfather's room?'

'It's ready. And there's nowhere else until the guests have gone.' Her only response was the lift of an eyebrow. 'It's not like that, Robbie.'

She shook her head. 'Leave your grandpa's room to me. I'll see to it.'

'Thank you.' Then, as Nancie pulled away from the bottle, wrinkled up her little nose, distancing herself from it, 'Have you had enough of that, sweetheart?'

She set the bottle on the table and just looked at her. She was so beautiful. Just like her mother.

'You'll need to wind her,' Robbie said. 'Put her on your shoulder and rub her back gently.'

'Oh, right.'

She lifted her, set her against her shoulder. Nancie didn't wait for the rub but obligingly burped. Before she could congratulate herself, she realised that her shoulder was wet and something warm was trickling down her back.

'Eeugh! Has she brought it all back up?'

'Just a mouthful. A little milk goes a very long way,' Robbie said, grinning as she handed her a paper towel. 'You used to do that all the time.'

'Did I?' No one had ever talked to her about what she was like as a baby. 'What did you do?'

'Changed my clothes a lot until I had the sense to put a folded towel over my shoulder before I burped you.'

'Well, thanks so much for the warning,' she said, using the towel to mop up the worst. 'What else did I do?'

'You cried a lot. You were missing your mother.'

Right on cue, Nancie began to grizzle and May stood up, gently rubbing her back as she walked around the kitchen.

'Poor baby. Poor Saffy.'

'So what did he tell you? What is this family crisis? Where is she?'

'Adam doesn't know. She dropped the baby off at his office and ran. He showed me the note she left with the baby, but she didn't sound quite in control, to be honest. It seems that Nancie's father has found out about her problems and he's trying to get custody.'

'In other words, he's pitched you into the middle of his family's messy life.'

'Saffy told him I would help.' Then, as she saw the question forming on Robbie's lips, 'He was desperate, Robbie.'

'Clearly, if he's prepared to marry you to get a babysitter.'

'My good luck.'

'Maybe. Do you remember that young jackdaw with the broken wing that he left on the doorstep?'

He'd left all kinds of creatures until Robbie had caught him and sent him packing. After that, he'd come over the park gate, dodging the gardener, keeping clear of the house, coming to look for her in the stables. She'd made him instant coffee while he'd emptied her biscuit tin, stayed to help her clean out the cages. It had been a secret. No one at home, no one at school had known about it. Only Saffy.

'I remember,' she said. 'What about it?'

'You cried for a week when it flew away.'

She swallowed. 'Is that a warning not to get too attached to Nancie?'

'Or her uncle.' She didn't wait for denial but, tapping the tip of her knife thoughtfully against the board, said, 'There's that old wooden cradle upstairs in one of the box rooms. You could use that for now. In fact, it might be a good idea to get Nancie out of here before the Christmas lot break for lunch.'

'Can you and Patsy manage?'

'Everything's done but the salad.' She jerked her head. 'Off you go.'

Well aware that Robbie could handle lunch with one hand tied behind her back, May returned to the peace of her sitting room, fastened Nancie into her buggy and went to find the old cradle.

When it was ready, she put it at the foot of her bed. 'Here you go, sweetie,' she said, putting down Nancie, then rocking her gently, humming the tune to an old lullaby to which she'd long since forgotten the words.

'Very pretty.'

She started, looked up.

Adam was leaning, legs crossed, arms folded, against the architrave of the door between her sitting room and bedroom. He'd abandoned the muddy pin-stripes for what looked like an identical suit, a fresh white shirt. Only the tie was different. It had a fine silver stripe that echoed the bright molten flecks that lifted his eyes above the ordinary grey.

'How long have you been standing there?' she demanded, hot with embarrassment.

'Long enough. Robbie directed me to the morning

room to wait for the lady of the house but, since I brought my bag with me, I decided to bring it up. Put it in my bedroom. I used the back stairs.'

'Don't be so touchy. She probably thought you'd blunder in and wake Nancie.'

'She's never seen me slip over the back gate and dodge the gardener.'

'No.' She looked away. It was the first time he'd alluded to the past. The golden days before she'd lied to her grandfather, lied to Robbie and gone to the school disco with him.

'How many generations of Coleridge babies have been rocked to sleep in that cradle?' he asked, pushing himself off from the door frame, folding himself up beside her.

'Generations,' she admitted. Probably even the children of the man whose unwillingness to settle down was causing her so much grief.

'Everything in this house looks as if it's been here for ever.'

'Most of it has. Unfortunately, there's one thing missing,' she said, scrambling to her feet, needing to put a little distance between them so that she could concentrate on what was important.

Kneeling shoulder to shoulder with him by the cradle she was far too conscious of the contrast between his immaculate, pressed appearance and her own.

He'd showered and smelled of fresh rain on grass, newly laundered linen. Everything clean, expensive.

She smelled of disinfectant, polish and the sicky milk that had dried on her shoulder. The band holding her hair back had collapsed so that it drooped around her face and she didn't need to check the mirror to know what that looked like. A mess.

'Nancie really should have a proper cot. Unfortunately I gave ours away. I'm going to have to run over to the baby store in the retail park after lunch and buy a few things. I can pick one up then.'

'We can get do that while we're out.'

'Out?'

'That's why I'm here. I've spoken to the Registrar. He can fit us in on the twenty-ninth.'

May opened her mouth. Closed it again. Then said, 'The twenty ninth?'

'Apparently, there have to be sixteen clear days from notice. That's the first day after that. He's free at ten o'clock. If that's convenient? It's a Monday. You haven't got anything planned for that day that you can't put off?'

She shook her head. 'We have mid-week courses and weekend courses, but Monday is always a clear day. What about you?' she asked.

'Nothing that won't keep for ten minutes,' he assured her. 'I assume you just want the basics?'

She hadn't given the ceremony any thought at all. Not since she was an infatuated teen, anyway, when she'd had it planned out to the last detail. But this wasn't an occasion for the local church scented with roses, choristers singing like angels and the pews packed with envious class mates as she swept up the aisle in a size 0 designer gown.

'The basics.' She nodded. 'Absolutely.'

'We'll need a couple of witnesses. Robbie, obviously. I thought we might ask Freddie Jennings to be the other one.'

'Good idea,' she said.

'I'm full of them today. All we need to do now is go to the office with our birth certificates and sign a few papers.'

'Now? But I can't leave Nancie.'

'Then you'll have to bring her along.'

'Yes. Of course,' she said, looking at Nancie. Looked at the buggy. Trying to imagine herself wheeling it through town with everyone thinking it was her and Adam's baby. 'I'd…um…better get changed.'

She grabbed the nearest things from her wardrobe. The discarded gold cord skirt and a soft V-necked black sweater, a fresh pair of tights from a drawer and backed into her bathroom. Where she splashed her face with cold water. Got a grip.

Because she was going to arrange her wedding and the Registrar would expect her to have made an effort, she put on some make-up, twisted her hair up into a knot, then stared at her reflection. Was that too much? Would Adam think she was making an effort to impress him?

Oh, for heaven's sake. As if Adam Wavell would care what she was wearing. And yet there was something so unsettling about the fact that he was in her home, sitting in her most private space, waiting for her.

It was too intimate. Too…

Nothing!

Absolutely nothing.

She wrenched open the door and he looked up, startled by the ferocity of her entrance.

Calm, Mary Louise. Calm…

'Okay?' he said.

'Fine. I just need my boots.' She took them from the closet, pulled them on, doing her best not to think about Adam standing at her bedroom window, Nancie against his shoulder.

'I'll just get my birth certificate and then we can go. I'll take Nancie if you'll bring the buggy.'

* * *

'Well, that was painless,' Adam said as they emerged from the register office.

May nodded, but she was very pale. And, while it might have been painless for him, everyone who worked in the Town Hall, the Registrar's Office, had known her. They'd been eager to congratulate her and cooed over the baby, assuming it was hers.

'Why did you let everyone think Nancie was your baby?' he said.

'I thought that it would be safer.'

'Safer?' He frowned.

'For Saffy.'

He was momentarily lost for words. While everyone knew her, she was an intensely private person and inside she must have been dying of embarrassment at being the centre of attention, but she'd smiled and smiled and let everyone think whatever they wanted in order to protect his wayward sister.

'I don't know about you, but I've missed lunch…' he said. 'Let's grab a sandwich.'

'I thought we were going to the business park. Nancie will need feeding again soon.'

'You won't be any use to her if you collapse from hunger,' he said, taking her arm, steering her across the road to the thriving craft centre that had once been a big coaching inn in the centre of the town.

It was lit up for the holiday season and packed with shoppers, but the lunch time rush was over in the court-yard café and they took a table near the window where there was room for the buggy.

'A BLT for me, I think. You?'

She nodded.

He ordered, adding a pot of tea without asking.

'You've had a shocking morning—we both have. Hot, sweet tea is what the doctor orders,' he said when the waitress had gone.

'The reality is just beginning to sink in.'

'It was a terrible thing to do to you,' he said.

'What? Oh.' She shook her head. 'His memory had gone. He didn't know.'

He'd assumed that she'd been talking about the loss of her home, but it seemed that marrying him was the shocker.

Well, if she'd been looking forward to an artistic partnership with the well-bred, public school educated but presumably penniless Jeremy Davidson—divorce would strip him of a large part of his assets—she had every reason to be in shock.

But, like her ancestor before her, she was prepared to do whatever it took to hold onto the family estate. Not so much a fate worse than death as a fate worse than being a nobody, living in an ordinary little house, the wife of a man who no one had ever heard of.

'Did you sort out your honey labels?' he asked.

She stared at him, then, as their food arrived, 'Oh, the labels. I took your advice and gave Jeremy the watercolour. He's going to scan it into his computer, see what he can do with it.'

Adam discovered he wasn't anywhere near as happy about that as he should have been, considering it had been his idea, but what could he say? That he didn't want the man in her bedroom, getting hot and sweaty at the thought of her peaches and cream body nestled in all that white linen and lace.

'My advice was to use a professional.'

'How much honey do you think I produce?' she

asked. 'I can't justify the kind of fees a professional designer would charge. Jeremy's doing it as a favour.'

'He's going to a lot of trouble to keep in with the school governor,' he said, pouring the tea. Loading it with sugar before handing her a cup. 'Is there a promotion in the offing?'

'Not that I know of.' She took a sip of the tea, pulled a face.

'Not sweet enough?' he asked and was rewarded with a wry smile that tugged at something deeper than the bitter memories.

'You are so funny,' she said, taking a dummy from the baby's carrier, unwrapping it and handing it to Nancie to suck.

'May…' His phone began to ring but he ignored it. Her relationship with Davidson was more important than whatever Jake wanted. If she thought that she could carry on—

May glanced up when Adam ignored his phone. 'Aren't you going to get that? It could be Saffy.'

'What?' He took the phone from his pocket, snapped, 'Yes,' so sharply that if she'd been Saffy she'd have hung up. Clearly it wasn't because, after a moment, he said, 'Fifteen minutes.' Then, responding to her expectant look, 'My office. I'm afraid I'll have to give the business park a miss. Can I have this to go, please?' he said, holding out his plate to the waitress before turning back to her. 'Let me have a list of what you need and I'll sort something out.'

'Get Jake to sort something out, don't you mean?' she said, edgy, although she couldn't have said why.

Just something about the way he'd looked at her, the way he'd said her name before his phone rang.

Was he having second thoughts?

'It's the same thing. He'll have to know where Nancie is in case Saffy turns up while I'm away next week. And you'll need someone to call on in the event of an emergency. He'll sort out a credit card for you as well.'

'I don't need your money, Adam.'

'Maybe not, but I understand from colleagues that babies are expensive and I don't expect you to subsidise my sister. With a card you can get whatever she needs.'

'She needs love, Adam, not a piece of plastic.'

'If you give her half as much as you lavished on your broken animals then she's in good hands,' he said. 'But it's not just Nancie. You'll need a wardrobe upgrade.' Before she could respond, he said, 'The sweats are practical, and the little black dress you've been wearing to every civic reception for the last five years is a classic, but when I present you to the world as my wife I will be looking for something a little more in keeping with my status.'

Presenting her…

His status…

Which answered any question about whether he'd changed his mind. He was going to marry her, but didn't want to be seen out with her until she'd had a makeover.

'Maybe you should consider an upgrade in your wife,' she snapped. 'Get one of those skinny blondes you're so fond of to take care of Nancie,' she continued, getting up so quickly that her chair scraped against the floor, causing heads to turn.

'Now who is there in the county who could outclass Miss May Coleridge?' he enquired, catching her hand.

The shock of the contact, the squeeze of his fingers around hers, warning her that she was in danger of making a scene, took the stuffing out of her knees and she fell back into her seat.

An unreadable smile briefly crossed Adam's face and it was there again. The feeling that she'd had just before he'd kissed her. Nothing that she could pin down. Just the realisation that this Adam Wavell was not the boy who'd trembled as he kissed her. He was a man who'd been thrown the smallest lifeline and within a decade had ousted the dead wood from an old family firm, seized control and built himself an empire. That took more than hard work, brains. It required ruthlessness.

She would have felt guilty about her part in flinging him the rope secretly begging an old family friend to give him a job, but for the fact that the family had come out of it with more money that they'd ever seen in their lives before.

'I was simply suggesting, with my usual lack of finesse,' he said when she didn't respond, 'that you might want to indulge yourself in some clothes for the Christmas party season.' He was still holding her hand just firmly enough to stop her from pulling away.

He'd always had big hands, all out of proportion to his skinny wrists, but they'd been gentle with animals. Gentle with her. The kind of hands you'd want to find if you reached out, afraid, in the dark.

He'd grown into them now. But were they safe?

'I'll ask Jake to give you a call next week so that he can go through the diary with you,' he said, with just enough edge to warn her that it was not up for discussion.

'Christmas parties should be the least of your worries,' she replied, refusing to submit. 'My only concern is Nancie. And Saffy. Have you done anything about finding her?'

He released her hand, took out his wallet and exchanged a bank note for the paper bag that the waitress offered him, telling her to keep the change.

'I've called a friend who runs a security company. Even as we speak, he's doing everything he can to trace her. And he's discreetly checking out what's happening in France, too.'

Oh, damn! Of course he was looking for her... 'I'm sorry,' she said, realising that she'd allowed her pride to override common sense. 'I didn't mean to snap at you.'

His hand rested on her arm for a moment in a gesture of reassurance. 'Forget it. Neither of us are having a good day.'

'Are you going to tell Jake everything?' she asked. 'I mean that you...me...we...' She couldn't say it.

'That you...me...we are going to get married?' he asked, smiling, but not unkindly, at her inability to say the words.

She nodded.

'It's a matter of necessity, May. I'm going to have to leave him to make all the arrangements.'

'Arrangements? What arrangements are involved in a ten-minute ceremony?'

He shrugged. 'Does it have to be ten minutes? I thought we might manage something a little more exciting than the Register Office.'

'Exciting? You think I need excitement?'

'Elegant, then. Somewhere where we can have lunch, or dinner afterwards so that I can introduce you to my directors and their wives.'

She opened her mouth. Closed it again.

'He'll sort out flowers, cars, photographs, press announcements. Arrange an evening reception for my staff.'

'You've given it quite a bit of thought.'

'I haven't had a baby to take care of.'

'No. It's just that I assumed... I thought...'

Adam had forgotten the way that he could read exactly what May was thinking. It had hit him with a rush when she'd lost it in the park, yelling at him for leaving Nancie, with everything she was feeling right there on her face. Nothing held back. All those years when she'd locked him out, avoided him had disappeared in the heat of it. The truth of it.

He could read her now as she tried to come to terms not with being married to him, but everyone knowing that she was his wife. Having to act out the role in public.

'You thought that no one need know?' he prompted, calling on years of hiding what he was thinking to disguise how that made him feel.

'I... Yes...' she admitted. 'It's a paper formality, after all. I didn't expect so much fuss. Show.'

'But that's the whole point of it, May,' he said gently. 'The show.' He'd got everything he wanted after all. And so had she. But both of them were going to have to pay. In his case, it would simply be money. In hers, pride. A fair exchange...'You wouldn't want the Crown Commissioners suspecting that you were just going through the motions to deny them Coleridge House, would you?'

'I thought asking Freddie Jennings to be a witness took care of that,' she said, her face unreadable. 'I'm sure it will make his day and once he gets home and tells his wife you needn't bother with a newspaper announcement. The news will be all around the town by nightfall.'

He didn't doubt it but the formality of an announcement in *The Times* was not something he intended to omit.

'I have to go. If you want a lift—'

'No. Thank you. I'll walk home. Introduce Nancie to the ducks.'

'Right. Well, I'll see you later. I don't know what time.'

She looked up at him, taking his breath away with an unexpected smile. 'If you're late, I'll do the wifely thing and put your dinner in the oven.'

Dinner? He'd never, in all his life, gone home to a cooked dinner. His mother's best effort was a pizza. Then it had been university and living on his own. Since his success, he was expected to be the provider of dinner in return for breakfast. At whatever restaurant was the place to be seen.

'What time do you eat?' he asked.

'It's a moveable feast. Seven?'

'I should be done by then.'

'Well, in case you're held up…' she opened the soft leather bag she carried over her shoulder, found a key fob '…you'd better have a key.' She sorted through a heavy bunch and, after hesitating over which one to give him, she unhooked a businesslike job and handed it to him. 'That's for the front door. I'll sort you out a full set before tomorrow.'

CHAPTER SEVEN

JAKE, being the perfect PA, didn't raise an eyebrow when Adam informed him that he was about to get married.

He simply listened, made a few notes and an hour later returned with a list of available wedding venues for May to choose from, a guest list for lunch and the reception and a draft of the announcement to go into *The Times*.

He scanned it, nodded. 'I mean to warn you that May will be calling with a list of things she needs for Nancie.'

'I've already spoken to Miss Coleridge. I needed her full name for the announcement in *The Times* and, since you were on a conference call—'

'Yes, yes,' Adam said with an unexpected jab of irritation as he realised, looking at the draft, that he hadn't known that her name was not May but Mary. Pretty obvious now that he thought about it. It was a month name and her birthday was in December...

'Show me the list.'

'It's a bit basic,' he said. 'I suggested a few things, but she insisted that was all she needed.'

She probably had most things, he realised. Like the antique cradle. When a family lived in the same house for generations nothing got thrown away. But she would have nothing new. Bright. Modern.

He'd made a mess of the clothes thing, but she wouldn't be able to refuse his insistence that she indulge Nancie. He wanted her to enjoy spending his money.

He wanted to make his mark on the house. Leave his imprint. Become part of the fabric of the house. Part of Coleridge history.

'Forget this, Jake,' he said. 'Call that big baby store on the business park and invite the manager to fulfil any new mother's wildest fantasies. Clothes, toys, nursery furniture. Just be sure that it's all delivered to Coleridge House before five o'clock today.'

Jake glanced at his watch. 'It's going to be tight.'

'I'm sure they'll find a way.'

'No doubt. I've ordered a credit card for May. It will be here on Monday. I'll deliver it myself.'

'A first class stamp will be quite sufficient,' he said. 'She isn't desperate.' Persuading her to use it would be the problem.

'It's no trouble. I have to pass Coleridge House on my way home and I can make sure that she's got everything she needs at the same time. I received the distinct impression, when I spoke to her, that Miss Coleridge isn't the kind of woman who would find it easy to pick up a phone to ask.'

'You're right. In fact, you might do worse than touch base with her housekeeper, Mrs Robson.'

When he'd gone, Adam sat back in his chair and turned to look out across the park to where the chimneys of Coleridge House were visible above the bare branches of the trees.

One phone call and Jake had got May's character down perfectly. She had never asked for anything. Never would. If Saffy hadn't sent him, reluctantly, in her direction today the first he—anyone—would have known about her loss would have been the 'For Sale' boards going up at the house.

Not that it would have been a totally lost opportunity. He could have bought it, moved his company in. Paved over the site of his humiliation and used it as a car park.

But that would not have been nearly as satisfying as the thought that tonight he'd sleep in James Coleridge's four-poster bed. And that in less than three weeks his granddaughter would become Mrs Mary Louise Wavell.

It took May a few moments to find her phone in the muddle of bags and boxes that had been piled up in her sitting room.

'Yes?' she snapped.

'You sound a little breathless, Mouse.'

'Adam...' She hadn't expected him to ring and if she hadn't been breathless from unpacking the cot, the sound of his voice would have been enough.

'I hope you're not overdoing it.'

'Overdoing it?' she repeated, propping the end of the cot with one hand, blowing hair out of her face. 'Of course I'm overdoing it. What on earth were you *thinking*?'

'I have no idea. Why don't you help me out?'

'I asked for a cot. One cot, a changing mat, a few

extra clothes and some nappies. What I've got is an entire suite of nursery furniture. Cupboards, shelves, a changing trolley with drawers that does everything but actually change the baby for you and enough nappies, clothes, toys for an entire…' he waited while she hunted for the word '…*cuddle* of babies!'

'A cuddle?' he repeated, clearly struggling not to laugh out loud. 'Is that really the collective noun for babies?'

'Cuddle, bawl, puke, poo. Take your pick.'

'Whoa! Too much information,' he said, not bothering to hide his amusement.

'I hate to be ungracious, Adam, but, as you can probably tell, I'm a bit busy.'

'You can leave the furniture moving until I get there.'

'Moving?' She looked around at the mess of packaging and furniture parts. 'This isn't just moving furniture, this is a construction project!'

'Are you telling me that it arrived flat-pack?'

'Apparently everything does these days.' She looked helplessly at the pile of shiny chrome bits that had come with the cot. 'And I have to tell you that I can't tell a flange bracket from a woggle nut.'

'Tricky things, woggle nuts,' he agreed.

'It's not funny,' she declared, but in her mind she saw that rare smile, the whole knee-wobbling, breath-stealing package… 'Is Jake there? He sounds a handy sort of man. Tell him if he can put this cot together I'll lavish him with Robbie's spiced beef casserole, lemon drizzle cake and throw in a slab of treacle toffee for good measure.'

'Jake is busy. I'm afraid you're going to have to manage with me.'

'You?'

'Do try to curb your enthusiasm, May.'

'No… It's just… I'm sorry, I didn't mean to sound ungrateful but I thought the whole point of this exercise was that you were *busy*. Up to your eyes in work. You couldn't even spare half an hour for lunch. Why are you calling, anyway?'

'I was going through the to-do list that Jake compiled for me and had just got to the rings.'

She lost control of the foot board of the cot, which she had been holding when the phone rang, and it fell against the arm of the sofa.

'May?' His voice was urgent in her ear.

'It's okay. Just a little flange bracket trouble.'

'Is there such a thing as a *little* flange bracket trouble?' he said, and she laughed.

Laughed!

How long was it since she'd done that?

'You've done this before,' she said.

'Once or twice,' he admitted. 'Actually, I called about the rings.'

'Rings?' The word brought her up with a jolt. 'No. I've got nuts, bolts, brackets,' she said, doing her best to turn it into a joke. Keep laughing. 'I can't see—'

'The wedding rings. I thought you'd want to choose your own.'

'No,' she said quickly.

'You're sure?'

'I meant no, you don't have to worry about it. I'll wear my grandmother's wedding ring.'

It was the ring she'd been going to wear when she married Michael Linton and took her place in society as a modern version of her grandmother. The perfect wife, hostess and, in the fullness of time, mother.

'I doubt your grandfather would be happy with the thought of me putting a ring he bought on your finger.'

'Probably not.' But it had to be better than picking out something that was supposed to be bought with love, 'forever' in your heart and pretending it was for real, she thought, the laughter leaking out of her like water from a broken pipe. 'But it's what I want.'

'Well, if you're sure.'

She was sure. Besides, if he bought her some fancy ring, she'd have to give it back but she could wear her grandmother's ring for ever.

'I am. Is that it?'

'No. There's a whole list of things you have to decide on, but they can wait until I've sorted out your flange thingies from your whatnots. Give me half an hour and I'll be with you.'

'It has to go there,' May declared, jabbing at the diagram with a neat unpolished nail.

They were kneeling on the floor of May's small sitting room, bickering over the diagram of a cupboard that did not in any way appear to match the pieces that had come out of the box.

He'd never noticed how small her hands were until he'd held them in his, soaping away the dirt of the park, applying antiseptic to her scratches. In the last couple of hours, as she'd held the pieces in place while he'd screwed the nursery furniture together—in between keeping Nancie happy—he'd found it increasingly difficult to concentrate on anything else.

'There is nowhere else,' she insisted.

Small, soft, pretty little hands that had been made to wear beautiful rings.

'I'd agree with you, except that you're looking at the diagram the wrong way up.'

'Am I? Oh, Lord, I do believe you're right.' She pulled off her glasses and sat back on her heels. 'That's it, then. I'm all out of ideas. Maybe it's time to admit defeat and call Jake.'

He looked up, about to declare that there wasn't anything that Jake could do that he couldn't do better, but the words died on his lips.

May had taken out her frustration on her hair and she looked as if she'd been dragged back, front and sideways through a very dense hedge. She was flushed with the effort of wrestling together the cot, then the changing trolley with its nest of drawers. None of which, despite the photographs of a smiling woman doing it single-handed on the instructions, she could ever have managed on her own.

But her butterscotch eyes were sparkling, lighting up her face and it was plain that, despite the frustration, the effort involved, she was actually enjoying herself.

And discovered, rather to his surprise, that he was too. Which, since it couldn't possibly have anything to do with constructing flat-pack furniture, had to be all about who he was constructing it with.

'You think I'm going to allow myself to be defeated by a pile of timber?' he declared.

'What an incredibly male response,' May said with a giggle that sucked the years away.

In all the frozen years he'd never forgotten that sound. Her smile. How it could warm you, lift your heart, make everything bad go away. No other woman had ever been able to do that to him. Maybe that was why he'd never been able to forgive her, move on. As far as the world was concerned, he'd made it; inside, he was still the kid who wasn't good enough...

'Anyone would think I was questioning your masculinity.'

'Aren't you?' He'd meant it as a joke but the words came out more fiercely than he'd intended, provoking a flicker of something darker in May's eyes that sent a finger of heat driving through his body and, without thinking, he captured her head and brought his mouth down on hers in a crushing kiss. No finesse, no teasing sweetness, no seduction. It was all about possession, marking her, making her pay for all the years when he couldn't get the touch of her hands on him, her mouth, out of his head.

He wanted her now, here, on the floor.

It was only Nancie's increasingly loud cries that brought him to his senses and, as he let her go, May stumbled to her feet, picked the baby up, laid her against her shoulder, shushing her gently to soothe her, or maybe soothe herself.

'I have to feed her,' she said, not looking at him as she made her escape.

Every cell in his body was urging him to go after her, tell her how he felt, what she did to him, but if he'd learned anything it was control and he stayed where he was until he was breathing normally.

Then he turned back to the cupboard, reread the instructions. Without the distraction of her hair, her hands, her soft and very kissable mouth just inches from his own, everything suddenly became much clearer.

May leaned against the landing wall, her legs too weak to carry her down the stairs, her hand pressed over her mouth. Whether to cool it or hold in the scalding heat of Adam's mouth on hers she could not have said.

It had been nothing like the kiss they'd shared that morning. That had been warm, tender, stirring up sweet desires.

This had been something else. Darker, taking not giving, and the shock of it had gone through her like lightning. She'd been unable to think, unable to move, knowing only that as his tongue had taken possession of her mouth she wanted more, wanted everything he had to give her. The roughness of his cheek, not just against her face, but against her breast. Wanted things from him that she had never even thought about doing with the man she had been engaged to.

She had been so aware of him all afternoon.

Adam had arrived, taken off his jacket and tie, rolled up his sleeves and her concentration had gone west as they'd worked together to construct the nursery furniture.

All she could think about was the way his dark hair slid across his forehead as he leaned into a screwdriver he'd had the foresight to bring with him.

The shiver of pleasure that rippled through her when his arm brushed against hers.

A ridiculous, melting softness as he'd looked up and smiled at her when something slotted together with a satisfying clunk.

When he'd grabbed her hand as she wobbled on her knees, held her until she'd regained her balance.

She'd just about managed to hold it together while they'd put together the cot. The changing trolley had been more of a challenge.

There were more pieces, drawers, and they'd had to

work more closely together, touching close, hand-to-hand close. She'd had the dizzying sensation that if she turned to look at him he would kiss her, would do more than kiss her. Would make all her dreams come true.

By the time they'd got to the cupboard her concentration had gone to pieces and she was more hindrance than help. She had been looking at the plan, but her entire focus had been on Adam. His powerful forearms. His chin, darkened with a five o'clock shadow. The hollows in his neck.

She'd felt as if she was losing her mind. That if she didn't escape, she'd do something really stupid. Instead, she'd said something really stupid and her dreams had evaporated in the heat of a kiss that had nothing to do with the boy she'd loved, everything to do with the man he'd become.

Adam was tightening the last screw when, Nancie fed and in need of changing, she could not put off returning to the nursery a moment longer.

'You did it!' she exclaimed brightly, forcing herself to smile. The reverse of the last years when she'd had to force herself not to smile every time she saw Adam.

'Once I'd got the woggle nuts lined up in a row,' he assured her as he tested the doors to make sure they were hanging properly, 'it was a piece of cake.'

'Would that be a hint?'

'Not for cake but something smells good,' he said, positioning a mini camera on top of the cupboard, angling it down onto the changing mat, where Nancie was wriggling like a little fish as she tried to undress her. 'This really is the business.'

'Amazing.' She leaned across to look at the monitor

at the same time as Adam. Pulled away quickly as her shoulder brushed against his arm. 'She's amazing.'

They were both amazing, Adam thought.

Throughout the afternoon he'd seen a different side to the shy, clumsy girl he'd known, the dull woman she'd become. He'd struggled to see her running a business that involved opening her home to strangers, putting them at their ease, feeding them.

'You'd be better off on your own,' she'd said, and he was about to agree when he'd realised that her hand, closed tightly over a runaway nut, was shaking.

He'd wrapped his hand over hers, intending only to hold it still while he recovered the nut, but her tremor transferred itself to him, rippling through him like a tiny shock wave, throwing him off balance, and he'd said, 'Stay.'

He'd been off balance ever since.

Totally lost it with a kiss that he could still see on her bee stung lips.

'What shall I do with all this packaging?'

'There's a store room in the stables,' she said as she eased Nancie out of her pink tights. 'Look, gorgeous, you're on television.'

Then, as she realised what she'd said, she glanced up at him and he saw her throat move as she swallowed, an almost pleading look in her eyes. Pleading for what? Forgiveness? Obliteration of memory?

'It's where we hold the craft classes,' she said quickly. 'They're always desperate for cardboard.'

Nancie made a grab for her hair and May, laughing, caught her tiny hand and kissed the fingers. As Adam watched her, the memories bubbled up. He'd kissed

May's fingers just that way. Kissed her lovely neck, the soft mound of her young breast.

A guttural sound escaped him and she turned, tucking the loose strand of hair behind her ear.

'Saffy is so lucky,' she said.

'Lucky?'

'To have Nancie…'

And as he looked into her eyes, he realised that the smile that came so easily to her lips was tinged with sadness.

Nearly thirty, she had no husband, no children, no life. Not his fault, he told himself. He'd come for her but she wanted this more than him. Well, he would give it to her. And she would finish what she'd started. Maybe in the hayloft…

'Is there any news of her? Saffy?' she prompted.

'Not yet,' he said abruptly, gathering a pile of flattened boxes and carrying them down into the yard, glad of the chill night air to clear his head.

It was pitch dark but the path and stable yard were well lit. There had been no horses here in a generation, no carriage for more than a century, but nothing much, on the outside, had changed.

The stable and carriage house doors shone with glossy black paint, wooden tubs containing winter heathers and pansies gave the area a rustic charm. A black and white cat mewed, rubbed against his legs.

There was even the smell of animals and a snort from the low range of buildings on the far side of the yard had him swinging round to where a donkey had pushed his head through the half door. A goat, standing on her hind legs, joined him.

The class had finished a while back. He'd heard cars

starting up, cheerful voices shouting their goodbyes to one another as he'd finished the cupboard. But the lights were on and a girl, busy sweeping the floor, looked up as he entered and came to an abrupt halt.

'Miss Coleridge is in the house,' she said.

'I know. She asked me to bring this out here.'

'Oh, right. You want the storeroom. It's down at the bottom. The door on the left.'

He'd expected to find the interior much as it had always been, still stables but cleaned up, with just enough done to provide usable work space.

He couldn't have been more wrong.

Serious money had been spent gutting the building, leaving a large, impressively light and airy workspace.

The loft had gone, skylights installed and the wooden rafters now carried state-of-the-art spotlights that lit every corner.

A solid wooden floor had been laid, there were deep butler's sinks along one wall, with wooden drainers and stacking work tables and chairs made the space infinitely adaptable. And, at the far end, the old tack room where they'd made coffee, eaten cake and shortbread, had been converted into bathroom facilities with disabled access. Everything had been finished to the highest standard.

Fooled by those useless labels, he'd assumed this was just a cosy little business that she'd stumbled into, but it was obvious that she'd been thinking ahead. Understood that there would be a time when Coleridge House would have to support itself, support her, if she was going to keep it.

He thought he knew her, understood her. That he was in control.

Wrong, wrong, wrong…

* * *

May settled Nancie, not looking up when Adam returned to collect the remainder of the packaging. Then, having angled the monitor camera on to Nancie in the cot, she went downstairs and checked the kitten, who she'd introduced to the kitchen cats, a couple of old sweethearts who were well used to stray babies—rabbits, puppies, even chicks, keeping them all clean and warm.

They'd washed him, enveloped him in their warmth and, as she stroked them, they licked at her, too. As if she was just another stray.

There was a draught as the back door opened and she turned as Adam came in.

'All done? Did you manage to cram everything in?'

'No problem. That's an impressive set-up you've got out there.'

She quirked an eyebrow at him. 'Did you imagine we just flung down some hay to cover the cobbles?'

'I didn't think about it at all,' he lied, looking around the kitchen rather than meet her eyes. Looking at the animals curled up in the basket by the Aga. The cats in the armchair, licking at the kitten. 'But now I'm wondering about the other side of your business. How you cater for your guests. Make your sweets. This is a very picturesque country kitchen, but I can't see it getting through a rigorous trading standards inspection for a licence to feed the paying public.'

'Oh? And what do you know about catering standards?'

'Amongst other things, my company imports the finest coffee from across the globe. It wouldn't look good if the staff had to go to a chain to buy their morning latte.'

'I suppose not.'

May knew, on one level, that Adam was hugely successful, but it was difficult to equate the boy who'd nicknamed her Danger Mouse, who'd always been around when she'd got into trouble, who'd stood outside this house, soaked and freezing, as he'd defied her grandfather, shouting out for her to go with him, as a serious, responsible businessman with the livelihood of hundreds, maybe thousands of people in his hands.

'How do you do it?' he asked, opening the fridge.

'Well, I had two choices,' she said, dragging herself out of the past. It was now that mattered. Today. 'What are you looking for?'

'A beer.' He pulled a face. 'My mistake.'

'You'll find beer in the pantry.' And, enjoying his surprise, 'Not all our workshops are women only affairs.'

'I'll replace it.'

'There's no need.'

'I'm not a guest.' And, before she could contradict him, he said, 'Can I get you anything?'

She shook her head. 'I'm babysitting.'

'Right.' He fetched a can from the pantry, popped it open and leaned back against the sink, watching as she donned oven gloves and took the casserole out of the oven. 'Two choices?'

'I could have torn this kitchen out, replaced it with something space age in stainless steel and abolished the furred and feathered brigade to the mud room, but that would have felt like ripping the heart out of the house.'

'Not an option.'

'No,' she said and, glad that he understood, she managed a smile. 'It was actually cheaper to install a second kitchen in the butler's parlour.'

Adam choked as his beer went down the wrong way. 'The butler's parlour?'

'Don't worry. It's been a long time since Coleridge House has warranted a butler,' she said and the tension, drum tight since he'd kissed her, dissipated as the smile she'd been straining for finally broke through.

'Well, that's a relief. It must still have been a major expense. Is it justified?'

'The bank seemed to think so.'

'The bank? You borrowed from the bank?'

May heard the disbelief in his voice.

'I suppose I could have borrowed from Grandpa,' she said. She'd had an enduring power of attorney. Paid the bills. Kept the accounts. Kept the house together. No one could have, would have stopped her. On the contrary. Grandpa's accountant had warned her that big old houses like this were a money sink and she needed to think about the future. Clearly, he hadn't known about the inheritance clause, either.

'Why didn't you?'

'It was my business. My responsibility.' Hers… Then, as she saw his horrified expression, 'You don't have to worry, Adam. I don't make a fortune, but I have enough bookings to meet my obligations. You won't have to bail me out.'

'What? No… I was just realising how much trouble you would have been in if I hadn't come along this morning. If I hadn't needed you so badly that I badgered you until you were forced to explain. You would have lost the lot.'

He wasn't thinking about himself? The realisation that, as her husband, he'd be responsible for her debts.

He was just thinking about her.

'It wouldn't have been the end of the world,' she said, putting the casserole on the table, the dish of potatoes baked in their jackets. Almost, but not quite. 'Once the contents of the house were sold, I'd have been able to pay them back.'

He caught her wrist. 'Promise me one thing, May,' he said fiercely. 'That, the minute you're married, you instruct Jennings to do whatever if takes to break that entailment.'

'It's number one on my list,' she assured him.

Not that there seemed much likelihood of her ever having a child of her own to put in this position. She hadn't thought much about that particular emptiness in her life until today when Nancie had clung to her, smiled at her.

'I'll have to make a new will, anyway. Not that there's anyone to leave the house to. I'm the last of the Coleridges.'

'No cousins?'

'Only three or four times removed.'

'They're still family and there's nothing like the scent of an inheritance to bring long lost relatives out of the woodwork.'

'Not to any purpose, in this case. I'll leave it to a charity. At least that way I won't feel as if I've cheated.'

'Cheated?'

'By marrying you just to keep the house.'

'You're not cheating anyone, May. If your grandfather hadn't had a stroke you would have been married to Michael Linton.'

'Maybe.' She'd been so very young and he'd been so assured, so charming. So *safe*.

That was the one thing she could never say about

Adam. Whether he was rescuing her from disaster, mucking out a rabbit cage or cleaning her wounds, as he had today, apparently oblivious to the fact that she was half naked, she had never felt safe with him.

Whenever she was near him she seemed to lose control of not just her breathing, but her ability to hold anything fragile, the carefully built protective barrier she'd erected around herself at school. One look and it crumbled.

She didn't feel safe, but she did feel fizzingly alive and, while he might not have noticed the effect he had on her, his sister hadn't missed it.

'You had doubts?' Adam asked, picking up on her lack of certainty.

'Not then.' At the time, marriage to Michael Linton had offered an escape. From her grandfather. From Maybridge. From the possibility of meeting Adam Wavell.

'And now?'

'Looking back, the whole thing seems like something out of a Jane Austen novel.'

'While your grandfather's will is more like something out of one of the more depressing novels of George Eliot.'

'Yes, well, whatever happens to the house in the future, it won't happen by default because I did nothing,' she assured him as she gestured for him to sit down. 'Actually, I'm sure the infallible Jake has it on his list but, just in case he'd missed it, you'll have to make a new will, too.'

'This is cheery.'

'But essential,' she said as she ladled meat onto a plate. 'Marriage nullifies all previous wills, which means that, should you fall under a bus—'

'Have you ever heard of someone falling under a bus?' he asked.

'Should you fall under a bus, the major part of your assets will come to me by default,' she persisted, determined to make her point. 'Not that I'd keep it,' she assured him. 'Obviously.'

'Why obviously?'

'You have a family.'

'There's always a downside,' he said, taking the plate. 'You'd get the assets, but you also get the bad debts.'

'Adam!'

'Would you entrust an international company to either my sister or my mother?' he demanded.

'Well, obviously—'

'They'd sell out to the first person who offered them hard cash, whereas you, with your highly developed sense of duty and the Coleridge imperative to hold tight to what they have, would be a worthy steward of my estate.'

She assumed he was teasing—although that remark about the Coleridges' firm grasp on their property had been barbed—but, as she offered him the dish of potatoes, his gaze was intent, his purpose serious.

'You'll get married, have children of your own,' she protested.

'I'm marrying you, Mary Louise. For better or worse.'

'That's a two-way promise,' May said, equally intent.

Adam held the look for long seconds, as if testing her sincerity, before he nodded and took the dish.

'Where's Robbie?' he asked, changing the subject. 'Isn't she eating with us?'

'It's quiz night at the pub,' she said, serving herself. Not that she had much appetite. 'She offered to give it a miss, but it's semi-final night and her team are red-hot.'

'She didn't trust me alone with you? What is she going to do? Sleep across your door?'

'Does she need to?' she asked flippantly, but as she looked up their eyes met across the table and the air hummed once more with a tension that stretched back through the years.

All the pain, the shame she'd masked from him each time, despite every attempt to avoid one another, they'd found themselves face to face in public. Both of them achingly polite, while he'd looked at her as if breathing the same air hurt him.

CHAPTER EIGHT

ADAM'S hand was shaking slightly as he picked up his fork. Robbie was no fool, he thought. She didn't trust him further than she could throw him and with good reason.

'Help yourself to another beer,' May prompted. 'Whatever you want.'

'I'm good, thanks,' he said, then, spearing a piece of carrot, 'I took a couple of carrots from the sack in the mud room and gave them to the donkey and his mate, by the way,' he said in a desperate attempt to bring things back to the mundane. 'I hope I didn't mess up their diet.'

'Everyone gets mugged by Jack and Dolly,' she said, clearly glad to follow his lead away from dangerous territory. 'They're a double act. Inseparable, couldn't be parted. And you're looking at the original mug. The one who took them both in.'

'I'll bet they didn't have to work anywhere near as hard as I did,' he said. 'One pitiful bleat from Dolly and I'll bet you were putty in their hooves.'

'Under normal circumstances I'd have been putty in yours,' she replied. And then she blushed. 'At least Jack keeps the paddock grazed.'

'Not Dolly?'

'She prefers bramble shoots, with a side snack of roses when no one's looking.' Maybe it was the mention of roses, but she leapt up. 'Nancie's awake,' she said, pushing back her chair, grabbing the monitor from the table. 'Help yourself,' she said, waving at the table. 'I've had enough.'

'Enough' had been little more than a mouthful, but she dashed from the room and he didn't try to stop her. Not because he believed the baby needed instant attention, but because suddenly every word seemed loaded.

He finished eating, cleared both their plates and stacked them in the dishwasher. Covered the food. Filled the coffee maker and set it to drip. Then, when May still hadn't appeared, he went upstairs to find her.

She was sitting in the dark, watching Nancie as she slept. The light from the landing touched her cheeks, made a halo of her hair.

'May?' he said softly.

She looked up. 'Adam. I'm sorry. I'm neglecting you,' she said, getting up and, after a last look at Nancie, joining him. 'There's leftover crème brulée in the fridge…'

'What happened to the lemon drizzle cake?'

'The Christmas course ladies finished it when they had tea. I'm sorry. It was always your favourite.'

'Was it? I don't remember,' he lied. 'I'm making coffee.'

'Well, good. You must make yourself at home. Have whatever you want. You'll find the drinks cupboard in the library.'

'Library?' He managed a teasing note. 'First a butler, now a library.'

'It's not a very big library. Do you want a tour of the house? I should probably introduce you to the ancestors.'

'If you're sure they won't all turn in their graves.'

She looked up at him and for a moment he thought she was going to say something. But after a pause she turned and led the way down a fine staircase lined with portraits, naming each of them as she passed without looking. But then, near the bottom, she stopped by a fine portrait of a young woman.

'This is a Romney portrait of Jane Coleridge,' she said. 'She's the woman who Henry Coleridge had his arm twisted to marry. The cause of all the bother.'

'You have the look of her,' he said. The same colouring, the same soft curves, striking amber eyes.

'Well, that would explain it,' she said, moving on, showing him the rest of the house. The grand drawing and dining rooms, filled with the kind of furniture and paintings that would have the experts on one of those antiques television programmes drooling. There was a small sitting room, a room for a lady. And then there was the library with its vast desk, worn leather armchairs.

She crossed to the desk and opened a drawer.

'These were Grandpa's,' she said, handing a large bunch of keys to him.

'What are they all?' he asked.

She took them from him and ran through them. 'Front, back, cellar—although we don't keep it locked these days. The gate to the park.' There were half a dozen more before she said, 'This one's for the safe.'

'The safe?'

She opened a false panel in one of the bookshelves to display a very old safe.

'Family documents, my grandmother's jewellery. Not much of that. She left it to my mother, and she sold most of it to fund Third World health care.'

Which was ironic, he thought, considering how she'd died. 'Her wedding ring? Can I see it?'

She shrugged. 'Of course.' She took the keys from him, opened the safe, handed him a small velvet pouch.

He wasn't sure what he'd expected. From her insistence that she wear it, he'd imagined something special, something worthy of a Coleridge, but what he tipped into his palm was a simple old-fashioned band of gold without so much as a date or initials inscribed on the inside.

It was a ring made to take the knocks of a lifetime. In the days when this had been forged, people didn't run to the divorce courts at the first hint of trouble but stuck to the vows they'd sworn over it.

'It's not fancy,' she said, as if she felt the need to apologise.

'It's your choice, May,' he said, wishing he'd insisted on buying a ring of his own. But he'd obliterate its plainness with the flash of the ring he'd buy to lie alongside it. He kept that to himself, however, afraid she'd insist on wearing her grandmother's engagement ring, too. Always assuming her mother hadn't sold that. He didn't ask, just removed the key to the back door and the park gate and added them to his own key ring, returning the rest to the drawer. 'Can I borrow it? So that I make sure my own ring matches it.'

There was just the barest hesitation before she said, 'Of course.'

'I'll take good care of it,' he assured her. 'Shall we have that coffee now? We have to make a decision on where we're going to hold the wedding.'

'There's a fire in the morning room. I'll bring it through.'

May took a moment as she laid the tray with cups, shortbread, half a dozen of the fudge balls she'd created for the Christmas market. Anything to delay the moment when she had to join him.

While she was with Adam, she was constantly distracted by memories, tripped up by innocent words that ripped through her.

Roses…

She'd never been able to see red roses without remembering Adam standing back from the door, shouting her name up at her window, oblivious to the approaching danger.

The bunch of red roses in his fist had exploded as her grandfather had turned the hose on him, hitting him in the chest and, for a terrible moment, she had thought it was his blood.

She'd tried to scream but the sound would not come through the thick, throat-closing fear that he was dead. It was only later, much later, when it was dark and everyone was asleep, that she'd crept outside to gather up the petals by the light of her torch.

Adam stretched out in front of the fire. His apartment was the height of luxury, everything simple, clean, uncluttered. It had been a dream back in the days when he'd been living in a cramped flat with his mother and his sister, the complete antithesis of this room, with its furniture in what could only be described as 'country house' condition. In other words, worn by centuries of use.

But the room had a relaxed, confident air. It invited

you to sit, make yourself comfortable because, after all, if you'd made it this far into the inner sanctum, you were a welcome visitor.

He leapt up as May appeared with a tray, but she shook her head and said, 'I can manage,' as she put it on the sofa table. 'Is it still black, no sugar?'

'Yes…' She remembered?

'Would you like a piece of Robbie's shortbread?' She placed the cup beside him. Offered him the plate. 'Or a piece of fudge?'

'These are the sweets you make?'

'This is a seasonal special. Christmas Snowball Surprise. White chocolate and cranberry fudge rolled in flaked coconut.'

He took one, bit into it and his mouth filled with an explosion of flavour, heat. 'You forgot to mention the rum.'

'That's the surprise,' she said, but her smile was weary and he saw, with something of a shock, that there were dark smudges beneath her eyes.

'Are you all right, May?' he asked when she didn't move, didn't pour herself a cup.

She eased her shoulder. 'I'm a bit tired. I think the fall has finally caught up with me.'

'Are you in pain?' he asked, crossing to her, running his hands lightly over her shoulder and she winced. 'You should have gone to Casualty. Had an X-ray.'

'It's just a strain,' she assured him. 'I'll be fine after a soak.' Then, before he could protest, 'I'm afraid the television is rather old, but it works well enough. And don't worry about security. Robbie will check the locks, set the alarm when she comes in.'

'Where is her room?' he asked.

That, at least, raised a smile from May. 'Don't worry.

You won't run into her in her curlers. She's got her own self-contained apartment on the ground floor.' She hesitated. 'You've got everything you need?'

He nodded, touched her cheek. 'Give me the monitor. I'll take care of Nancie if she wakes.'

'No. You've got a long flight tomorrow. You'll be in enough trouble with jet lag without having a sleepless night.'

'That's why I'm here,' he said.

'Is it?' She pushed a hand distractedly through her hair, as if she'd forgotten his promise to take the night shift. 'There's no need for that. You've done your hero stint with the furniture. What time are you leaving?'

'The car will pick me up at nine.'

'I hadn't realised you were leaving so early.' She looked at the coffee on the tray in front of her. 'Another half an hour—'

'There'll be plenty of time to sort out the wedding details over breakfast. Go and soak your aches.'

Adam couldn't sleep. He'd hung his suit in the great oak wardrobe made from trees that had been growing in the seventeenth century.

Tossed his dirty linen in the basket. Soaked a few aches of his own away in the huge roll-top Victorian bath, no doubt the latest thing when it had been installed. Having a fully grown woman fall on you left its mark and he'd found a bruise that mirrored May's aches on his own shoulder.

Then he'd stretched his naked limbs between the fine linen sheets on the four-poster bed, lay there, waiting for the sense of triumph to kick in. But, instead, all he could think about was May.

May not making a fuss, even though she'd clearly been in pain.

May trembling when he touched her. The hot, dark centre of her eyes in the moment before he'd kissed her. Wishing he was lying with his arms around her amongst the lace and frills, instead of the icy splendour of James Coleridge's bed.

The phone startled May out of sleep and she practically fell out of bed, grabbing for it before it woke Nancie.

'Hello?'

'May…'

'Saffy! Where are you? Are you safe?'

'I'm okay. Is Nancie all right?'

'She's fine. Gorgeous, but what about you? Where are you? Why didn't you come straight to me? You know I'd have helped you.'

'I wasn't sure. It's been a long time…'

'Come now. Adam's desperate with worry. Let me get him—'

'He's there?'

'He's staying with Nancie,' she said, keeping it simple. Explanations could wait. 'Saffy? Saffy, I've got plenty of room. You should be with Nancie,' she said quickly. But, before she'd finished, she was talking to herself.

She dialled one four seven one, to find out what number had called but the number had been withheld.

'There was no point in disturbing you,' May protested in response to his fury that she hadn't bothered to come and tell him that his sister had called in the night. 'There was nothing you could do.'

In contrast to the quiet of his own apartment first thing, the kitchen was bedlam. Nancie grizzling on May's shoulder, the chicken was squawking at the cats, the dog was barking and there was some schmaltzy Christmas song on the radio. He reached out and switched it off.

'That's not the point.'

He'd spent most of the night lying awake, then when he had fallen asleep, he'd been plagued by dreams he couldn't remember, overslept. He felt like a bear with a sore head and apparently it showed because she stuck a glass of orange juice in his hand.

'Here. Drink that.'

He swallowed it down and took a breath. The last thing he was going to tell her was that she wouldn't have been disturbing him. If she knew that he'd been lying awake, had heard the phone, she'd want to know why he hadn't come to check for himself.

He could hardly tell her that he'd lain in James Coleridge's hard bed imagining some private middle of the night exchange between her and Jeremy Davidson.

Imagining her reassuring him that her marriage would only be a paper thing. That in a year she'd be free. That if they were discreet...

Because that was what lovers did. Called one another in the small hours when they couldn't sleep.

It hadn't crossed his mind that it would be Saffy. He hadn't been thinking about her at all, he realised. Or his baby niece, crying for her mother.

May had accused him of thinking only about himself and she was right.

'Here, give her to me,' he said, taking the baby, holding her at arm's length. Shocked out of her misery, she stared back him, her cheeks flushed, her black curls in disarray, a beauty in the making. His sister's child.

There and then he made her a silent promise that, whatever happened, he would ensure that her life was very different from that of her mother. That she would always know she was cherished, loved.

She gave a little shudder.

'Don't fret, sweetheart,' he said, putting her against his shoulder. 'We'll find your mother, but in the meantime May is doing her best so you must be good for her while I'm away.' He looked down at her. 'Do we have a deal?'

'She'll dribble on your shirt,' May warned as she clutched at him, warm and trusting.

'It'll sponge off.' Then he frowned. 'How did Saffy get your number? It's unlisted.'

'I gave it to her once. I'm sorry. If she calls again…' She stopped as she caught sight of his grip, his laptop bag. 'Maybe it's as well that you won't be here. She hung up when I said I'd get you.'

It sounded like a reproach. And, if it was, he deserved it. He'd worked so hard to distance himself from his family that now his sister was frightened to come to him.

'If she rings again, I'll do my best to persuade her to come here,' she said, then, as the doorbell rang, she glanced at the clock. 'Oh, Lord, that's your car and you haven't had any breakfast. I'm not usually this disorganised.'

'You don't usually have a baby to look after. Don't worry; I'll get something at the airport. If you need anything, you've got Jake's number. He'll know how to get in touch.' He kissed Nancie, surrendered her to

May. 'We never did get around to deciding where to hold the wedding.'

'Does it matter?' she asked. Then, maybe realising that was less than gracious. 'Why don't we leave it to Jake? Let him surprise us.'

'If that's what you want.' He picked up his bags and she made to follow him, but he said, 'Don't come to the door. Stay in the warm.'

'You will be careful, Adam?'

'I'll watch out for low flying buses,' he said flippantly.

After he'd gone everything went quiet. The chicken, stupid thing, stopped tormenting the cats who, embarrassed, settled down to give each other and the kitten a thorough wash. The dog dropped his head back on his paws. Nancie sighed into her shoulder.

It was quiet, peaceful and if all the tension had gone out of the room, out of the house with Adam, he'd taken all the life with him, too.

Abandoning any thought of breakfast, she took Nancie upstairs. 'Okay, little one. This is going to be an adventure for both of us,' she said as she filled the baby bath, checked the temperature. 'Now, promise you'll be gentle with me.'

Ten minutes later, and considerably damper, she wrestled the baby into a pair of the sweetest pink velvet dungarees, then put her down in the cot and turned on the musical mobile.

She'd just finished mopping up the bathroom and changed into dry clothes when Robbie put her head around the door.

'Is the coast clear?'

'Sorry?'

'Has he gone?'

'Adam? Yes. Half an hour ago. And where were you hiding when I needed you? I've never bathed a baby in my life.'

'Then it's time you learned how. I was feeding the livestock and just look what I found sharing Jack and Dolly's bed of hay.'

She opened the door wider to reveal a shivering and sorry looking woman, bundled up in a thick coat, head-scarf and peering at her through heavy-framed glasses.

She looked vaguely familiar... The woman in the park yesterday. She took off the glasses and pushed the scarf back to reveal glossy black hair and said, 'Hello, May.'

'Saffy!'

'I'll go and make some tea,' Robbie said, leaving them to it.

'I saw you. Yesterday.'

'I didn't mean to stay. I was going back to France, to confront Michel. I just wanted to be sure that he was bringing Nancie to you but the idiot left her on the path where anyone could have taken her...'

'That's what I said. I shouted at him.'

'Did you?' That made her smile. 'You were always shouting at him. That's how I knew you liked him,' she said. 'It's why I twisted his arm, forced him to ask you to the disco that night. You'd been so kind...' Then, 'I just wanted you to have a good time.'

'I know. Nothing that happened was your fault.' It had been hers. If she'd been braver, instead of hiding her friendship with Adam, if her grandfather had been given a chance to get to know him... 'Have you been out there all this time?'

Saffy nodded and May frowned. 'But I don't understand. If you were going to see Michel…'

'I lost my nerve. I thought I might be arrested. That the police might be watching for me at Adam's office. In the end I wandered around for a bit. Bought some food. I stayed in the library for a long time. It was late night closing. I spent as long as I could eating a burger to stay in the warm.'

'Why on earth didn't you come to me?'

'Because I'm wanted by the authorities. I didn't want to get you into trouble.'

'Oh, for goodness' sake, come here,' she said, holding out her arms and gathered her in, holding her tight.

'I tried to sleep in the park, but it was so cold and I when I tried your gate it was unlocked and I thought, maybe you wouldn't mind but when you said Adam was here… He's going to be so angry with me…'

'Not half as angry as I'm going to be with him,' she said.

Then, standing back, 'Saffy Wavell, you stink of goat. Out of those things and into the bath with you before you go anywhere near your gorgeous little girl.'

Adam had just reached the airport when his phone rang. It was number withheld. 'Saffy?'

'Adam—'

'May…' He'd been trying to block out the scene in her kitchen. Noisy, alive, full of warmth and life, a total contrast to his own sterile existence.

He hadn't lacked for female company, but he dated women who were more interested in being seen in the gossip magazines than in anything more domestic than opening a bottle of champagne. The kind of women that his sister had always wanted to be. Tall, beautiful but, despite May's accusation, not always blonde. The colour of their hair hadn't mattered. The only unchangeable requirement was that they didn't remind him of her.

But the unexpected sound of her voice against his ear brought her so close that he felt as if she were touching him.

Just one day in her company and he was in danger of falling under the spell she'd cast on him when he was too young to protect himself from the kind of pain that brought. Forgetting what this was about.

'Is there a problem?' he asked, keeping his voice cool.

'No. I only wanted to let you know that Saffy's here with me. That she's safe.'

Relief flooded through him. Gratitude. He held it in. 'You were right, then. She wasn't far away. Can I talk to her? Or is she determined to avoid me?'

'She's in the bath right now and then I'm going to feed her and put her to bed.'

'I'll take that as a yes.' Well, what did he expect? He'd kept her at arm's length for years. She knew he didn't want her around, reminding people who he was. Where he came from. 'I'll see what I can do about damage limitation,' he said. 'I'll get Jake to organise a family lawyer.' He could do that for her. 'Try and sort out the mess.'

'It's the weekend. Nothing is going to get done until Monday. Let me talk to her, Adam. Find out what's happened. If it can't be straightened out, I'll call Jake myself.'

'Damn it—'

'Your priority is your trip, Adam. And there's no harm in trying honey before we go for the sting.'

'You should know.' But she was undoubtedly right. In cases like this, soft words might well prove more effective than going in heavy-footed. Something that he wouldn't have had to be told if this was a business negotiation. But his family had never been exactly good when it came to relationships. 'Try it your way first, but tell Saffy she has to stay with you until I get back.'

'Oh, that will work.'

'May! I'm concerned about her. Please ask her to stay with you until I get back.'

'Better.'

'What is this, family relationship counselling?' She didn't answer. 'Tell her that I'm not angry, okay. That I'm glad she's safe.'

'Wow.'

'Sarcasm does not become you, Miss Coleridge.'

'Forget she's your sister, Adam. Think of her as some frightened creature that you've found,' she said, using his own words to her when he'd been trying to persuade her to take Nancie. 'It's in pain and you've picked it up and brought it to me.'

'Damn it!' Was she mocking him? 'Do whatever you want,' he said and hung up.

Around him, the terminal buzzed with people wheeling heavy suitcases as they searched for their check-in desks. They were harassed but excited, looking forward to going on holiday or to stay with family.

He had a sister and a mother who he kept at arm's length. Out of sight, out of mind. He had no one. No one except May. He looked at the phone in his hand, scrolled down to her number.

'Adam?'

From the way she said his name, he suspected that she hadn't moved, but had been waiting for him to call back. And he couldn't make up his mind whether the feeling that ripped through him was anger that she could read him that well or an ache for something precious that had been trampled on, destroyed and was lost for ever.

'You can tell my sister,' he said, 'that, whatever happens, she can count on me. That I won't let her down. That I won't let anyone take Nancie away from her.'

'And that you won't shout at her?' she insisted, but now there was a smile in her voice.

'You're one tough negotiator, Danger Mouse. I don't suppose you'd reconsider that job offer?'

'As a nanny? I'm already redundant.'

'If you think that, you're in for a rude awakening. You now have two babies to take care of.' She didn't say a word and, after a moment, he laughed.

'Okay. I'll do my best, but you'll have to stand very close so that you can jab me with your elbow if I forget.'

'My elbow? My pleasure,' she said, but she was laughing too and he was glad he'd called.

'I have to go.'

'Yes. Please be careful, Adam.'

'May…'

'Yes?'

There was a long pause while a hundred possibilities rushed into his head.

'I'll call you in the morning. Maybe you'll have got some sense out of Saffy by then.'

CHAPTER NINE

MAY surrendered her room to Saffy so that she was next to the nursery, loaning her a nightdress since she didn't seem to have any luggage. Sorting her out some clothes.

She slept most of the day, waking only when Nancie cried to be fed, the pair of them curled up in bed together.

She and Robbie worked quietly, stripping the bedrooms, getting them ready for the next group of guests who would be arriving the following Friday for a three-day garden design course. Then she took Nancie for a walk, sticking up posters with a picture of the kitten to the lamp posts in the park on her way in to Maybridge to pick up some underwear for Saffy who, despite having given birth recently, was still at least two sizes smaller than her.

Keeping herself busy, counting off the long hours until Adam's flight landed.

By the evening, Saffy had recovered. Robbie announced she was going to the cinema with a friend, leaving them to spend the evening catching up.

'I really love Michel,' she said after she'd given

chapter and verse on how they'd met. How handsome he was. How romantic. 'It's his mother. She never liked me. She is such a snob. She's done everything she can to split us up and when that didn't work she dug up all that stuff from when I was a kid. Telling Michel that I was a danger to Nancie. That I couldn't be trusted.'

'Did he ask you about it?'

'Of course and I told him everything. Not that I nearly went to jail. That you saved me. But everything else,' she said.

'You can't hide, Saffy. Michel has rights, too. And you've put yourself in the wrong. He must be frantic with worry. Not just for the baby,' she added.

'I was frightened.'

'Of course you were. Do you think it would help if I spoke to him? Explained?'

It took a while to persuade her but, an hour later, a sobbing Saffy was talking to Michel, declaring how much she loved him.

Adam finally rang at ten the following morning.

May, in an unfamiliar bed, had scarcely slept and jumped every time a phone rang. Once it had been Jake, to let her know that Adam had arrived safely just after ten the previous evening and to ask if she needed anything.

Mostly it was Michel calling Saffy to mutter sweet nothings. Clearly the thought of losing her had brought him to his senses.

'I tried earlier, but the line was engaged.'

'It's the French lover.'

'They're talking?'

'Endlessly. I've suggested he comes to stay but, from his reluctance, I suspect he hasn't told his parents that they're reunited. *Maman* sounds like a dragon.'

'There are worse things than an over-protective mother.'

'True.'

'I'm sorry, May. At least I had one.'

'Forget it. How was the flight?'

'Long. Boring. I'd seen the film. The food was terrible. Pretty much what you'd expect.'

'Well, you've got that Presidential dinner to look forward to.'

'Not until the end of the week.' He told her his itinerary; she gave him her mobile number. 'I have to go, May. I'll call you later. Take care.'

'Take care,' she repeated softly when he'd hung up, holding the phone to her breast.

He called every morning on the landline and talked, not just to her, but Saffy. Called every evening on her mobile when she was in bed. She updated him on the saga of the French lover and his mother. He told her what he'd been doing. Nothing of any importance. The words weren't important. It was hearing his voice.

May, up to her eyes preparing for the arrival of a houseful of guests as well as preparing a rush order of fudge, snatched the phone off the hook.

It was the tenth time it had rung that morning. The announcement of their forthcoming wedding had appeared in *The Times* that morning and she'd been inundated with calls. Only Adam hadn't rung.

'Yes!' She snapped as snatched up the phone.

'Whoa. Bad morning?' Adam said, making the whole hideous morning disappear with a word.

'You could say that.' But not now... 'I'm just busy. Michel and his parents are arriving this afternoon.'

'His parents?'

'It was my idea to invite them. He's finally owned up to his *maman* that the relationship is back on and he wants to marry the mother of his child.'

'Not before time.'

'His mother still thinks that Saffy is a scheming little nobody with a bad history who's not fit to clean her boy's boots, let alone raise her grandchild. I'm going to change her mind. Prove to her that the Wavells have connections. Robbie and Saffy are polishing the family silver even as we speak.'

'You're giving them the full country house experience?'

'Absolutely. The best crystal, the Royal Doulton, Patsy in a white apron waiting table. I'm even going to wear my grandmother's engagement ring. Just to emphasize that Saffy is about to become my sister-in-law.'

There was a silence, a hum on the line and for a moment she thought she'd lost the connection.

'Your mother didn't sell that?'

'It's been in the family for ever. Jane Coleridge is wearing it in the Romney portrait, something I'll point out when I introduce them to the ancestors. Knock them out with centuries of tradition.'

'Just as long as they don't think that I'm too cheap to buy you one of your own.'

'Adam...'

'You've clearly got everything under control, there.

I'll call later and see if you've managed to cement the entente cordiale.'

He rang off. May replaced the receiver rather more slowly. Clearly he'd been annoyed about the ring but there was no point in worrying about it.

If she was going to hit them with afternoon tea in the drawing room, install Michel's parents in state in the master bedroom and then serve the kind of traditional British food at dinner that would make a Frenchman weep with envy, she didn't have a minute to spare.

'Did I wake you?'

'No.' May had snatched up the phone at the first hint of a ring, on tenterhooks, not sure that he'd ring. 'I've just this minute fallen into bed. I wanted to lay up for breakfast in the conservatory before I turned in.'

'How did it go?'

'My face is aching from smiling,' she admitted. In truth, every muscle was throbbing, more from the tension than the effort. Catering for charity lunches, receptions, had been part of her life for as long as she could remember but so much had been riding on this. 'But in a good cause. I think Michel's *maman* is finally convinced that Saffy's youthful indiscretions were no more than high jinks.'

'If she believes that, you must have done some fast talking.'

'The fact that Grandpa was a magistrate was the final clincher, I think. And maybe the four-poster bed.'

'You put them in *my* bed?'

'In the state bedroom,' she said, chuckling. 'I dug out a signed picture that the Prince of Wales gave my great-grandfather in 1935 and put it on the dressing table.'

'Nice touch.'

'And then, of course, we wheeled out the family star.'

'Nancie?'

'Well, she played her part. But I was actually talking about you. *Maman* had no idea that Saffy's brother was the billionaire Chairman of the company whose coffee she cannot, she swears, live without.'

'Oh.'

'A double whammy. Class and cash. How could she resist? Whether you'll thank me when you've got them as in-laws is another matter. Michel and his father are both gorgeous to look at, but totally under the matriarchal thumb.'

'Why, May?'

She'd been snuggling down under the duvet, warm, sleepy and this morning's misunderstanding forgotten, loving the chance to tell him about her triumph on his behalf.

'Why what?' she asked.

'Why would you go to so much trouble for Saffy?'

'I wasn't…' She wasn't doing it for Saffy; she was doing it for him.

'Don't be coy. You've pulled out all the stops for her. What is it between you two?'

'She never told you?'

'My little sister lived for secrets. It gave her a sense of power.'

'I was being bullied. When I first went to the High School. A gang of girls was taking my lunch money every day. They cornered me, took my bag and ripped pages out of my books until I gave them everything I had.'

'Why on earth didn't you tell someone? Your year head?'

'The poor little rich girl running to teacher? That would have made me popular.'

'Your grandfather, then?'

'His response would have been to say "I told you so" and take me away. He'd always wanted to send me to some fancy boarding school.'

'Maybe you should have gone. I never got the impression you enjoyed school much.'

'I didn't. But I couldn't bear to be sent away. I didn't have a mother or a father, Adam. All I had was my home. The animals.'

Coleridge House. And a cold man who probably hated having a love-child for a granddaughter.

'What made you go to Saffy?' he asked.

'I didn't. I don't know how she found out. But one day she was at the school gate waiting for me. Didn't say a word, just hooked her arm through mine as if she was my best friend. To be honest, I was terrified. I knew they'd all gone to the same primary school.'

'It was pretty rough,' he admitted.

'Well, I thought it was some new torture, but she appointed herself my minder. Walked me in and out of school, stayed with me at lunch and break times until they got the message. I was protected. Not to be touched.'

'That's why she knew you'd take Nancie? Because you owed her.'

'No. I paid my debts in full a long time ago...' She stopped, realising that, tired, she'd let slip more than she'd intended. 'Ancient history,' she said dismissively. 'Tell me about your day, mixing with the great and good. There was something about Samindera on the news this evening, but it was a bit of a madhouse and I didn't catch it.'

'Well, obviously the fact that I had dinner with the President would make the national news,' he said.

'There's nothing wrong?' she persisted.

She'd meant to check but, by the time she'd finished, she was fit for nothing but a warm bath and bed.

'His Excellency's hand was steady enough on his glass,' he assured her.

'Oh, well, what can possibly be wrong? Tell me what you ate,' she asked, then lay back as he told her about the formal dinner, the endless speeches, apparently knowing exactly what would make her laugh. Then, as her responses became slower, he said, 'Go to sleep, Mouse. Tell Saffy that I'll call her in the morning. And that I'll want to talk to Michel when I get home.'

'How long? Three days?' It had been nearly two weeks since she'd seen him, but it felt like a lifetime. 'Are you going to play the big brother and ask him his intentions?'

'I think he's already demonstrated his intentions beyond question. I just want to be sure that this is settled and it's not going to end in some painful tug of love scenario. Saffy might be an idiot, but she's my sister and no one is going to take her baby from her.'

'Actually, she was talking about going back with them tomorrow.'

'Show her my credit card. Ask her to go shopping with you. That should do it.'

'Too late. She's dragged me out shopping half a dozen times, although I'm not sure if it's my trousseau she's interested in or her own.'

'I hope you've been indulging yourself rather than her.'

'She's a very bad influence.' she admitted.

'That sounds promising.'

She'd been led utterly astray by his sister, and now possessed her own sexy 'result' shoes with ridiculously high heels. And had rather lost her head in an underwear shop. Not that she anticipated a result. Adam had been very quick to make it clear that this was a marriage in name only, but at least she'd *feel* sexy. And taller.

'Just make sure she knows that I want to see her. And my mother. That I want to make things right.'

'No problem. I've invited them all to the wedding.'

There was a pause. Then he said, 'Let's elope.'

Adam sat on the edge of the bed, her giggle a warm memory as he imagined her slipping into the warm white nest of her bed, already more asleep than awake.

She wouldn't have let it slip that she'd already paid her debt to his sister if she'd been fully awake. Even then, she'd done her best to cover it, move on before he pressed her to tell him what she'd done. But he hadn't needed to. He knew.

Saffy had been caught with several tabs of E in her bag when the police had raided a club a few days before his and May's big night out had been brought to an abrupt end in the hayloft.

It wasn't the first time his sister had been in trouble. She'd been caught shoplifting as a minor, drinking underage, all the classic symptoms of attention seeking. But this had been serious.

She'd sworn she'd got the tabs for friends who'd given her the money, but technically it was dealing and she was older. Culpable. But she'd shrugged when he'd found out, gone ballistic at her stupidity. Said it was sorted. And then, two weeks later, when she'd been summoned to the police station, she'd got away with no more than a formal caution. It would be on her record, but that was it.

That was what May had done. She'd talked to her grandfather, pleaded Saffy's case. And left them both wide open to the retribution of a hard old man.

What had he threatened?

What had she surrendered?

School. She'd never come back. The rumour was that she'd gone off to some posh boarding school and he'd allowed himself to believe it, hope that was what had happened, why she hadn't called him, written. Until he'd seen a photograph of her in the local newspaper, all dressed up at some charity do with her grandfather. Surrounded by Hooray Henrys in their DJs.

And him, he thought. She'd given up him to save Saffy from the minimum of three months in prison she'd have got at the Magistrates' Court. Much more if the Bench had decided the case was too serious for them and sent it up to the Crown Court. Which he didn't doubt would have happened.

No. That was wrong.

He dragged his hands through his hair. He was only seeing it from his point of view. How it had affected him.

Narrow, selfish…

May had surrendered herself. Given up every vestige of freedom for his sister. And maybe for him, too. He hadn't broken any laws, couldn't be got at that way. But he'd had an offer from Melchester University. He'd been encouraged to apply to Oxford, but he needed to be near enough to take care of his mother and sister. He had no doubt James Coleridge could have taken that from him.

Was that what May had been trying to tell him as

she'd stood at her window shaking her head as he'd called her name?

Watching while the hose had been turned on him, smashing the roses he'd bought her in an explosion of red petals...

He groaned, slid from the bed to the floor as he remembered picking up the book of *Sonnets*. That was what had fallen from it. The petal from a red rose. He'd recognised it for what it was and brushed it off his fingers as if tainted...

Stupid, stupid...

If, that first time when their paths had crossed at some civic or charity reception, he'd forgotten his pride and, ignoring the frost, reached out and taken her hand, how long would she have held out?

He'd assumed that he'd caught her offside up that tree, but maybe that was all it would have taken. A smile, a, *Hello, Danger Mouse*, a touch to melt the icy mask.

But pride was all he'd had and he'd clung to it like ivy to a blasted oak.

He had to talk to her. Now. Tell her that he was sorry...

The phone dragged May back from the brink of sleep. She fumbled for it, picked it up. Couldn't see the number without her glasses. 'Hello?'

'May...'

'Adam? Is something wrong?'

'No... Yes...'

She heard a noise in the background. 'What was that? I heard something...'

'Thunder, lightning. Storms are ten a penny here. Are you awake?'

'Yes,' she said, pushing herself up. 'What is it? What's wrong?'

'Everything... Damn it, the lights have gone out.'

'Adam? Are you okay?'

'Yes. That happens, too. It doesn't matter...' He broke off and she could hear shouting, banging in the background.

'Adam!'

'Hold on, there's some idiot hammering on the door. Don't go away. This is important—'

Whatever else he was going to say was drowned out by the sound of an explosion. And then there was nothing.

Robbie found her sitting, white-faced, frozen in front of the television, watching rolling news of the attempted coup in Samindera. Pictures of the Presidential Palace, hotels blackened by fire, shattered by shells.

Reports of unknown casualties, missing foreigners. The fierce fighting that was making communication difficult.

She fetched a quilt to wrap around her, lit the fire, made tea. Didn't bother to say anything. She knew there was nothing she could say that would mean a thing.

Jake called on his way into the office, where the directors had called a crisis meeting, promising to let her know the minute he heard anything.

The French contingent finally emerged, then, when they heard the news, they hugged both her and Saffy a lot, talking too fast for May's schoolgirl French but clearly intent on reassuring her that they were all family now.

Michel sat holding Saffy's hand, their baby on his

lap, watching the news with her. And that made her feel even more alone.

She leapt up when the phone rang, but it was Freddie. He'd seen the forthcoming wedding announcement in *The Times*.

'There isn't going to be a wedding,' she said and hung up.

'May!' Saffy looked stricken. 'Don't say that. Adam's going to be all right.'

'No. He isn't.' She wrapped her arms around herself, staring at the same loop of film that was being rerun on the television screen, rocking herself the way she'd done as a child when her dog had died. 'He phoned last night. I was talking to him when…' She couldn't say it. Couldn't say the words. 'I heard an explosion. Right there, where he was. He's dead. I know he's dead and now he'll never know. I should have told him, Saffy.'

'What? But you said you were marrying him to save the house? That it was just a paper arrangement.' Then, as reality dawned, she said, 'Oh, drat. You're in love with him.'

May didn't answer, but collapsed against her and, as she opened her arms and gathered her in, shushed her, rubbing her back as if she were a baby.

When Adam regained consciousness he was lying face down in the dark. His ears were ringing, the air was thick with choking dust.

As he pushed himself up, leaning back against something he couldn't see, a nearby explosion briefly lit up the wreckage of his room and the only familiar thing was the cellphone he was clutching in his hand.

He'd been talking to May. He'd had something important to tell her but someone had been hammering on the door...

He put the phone to his ear. 'May?' He began to choke as the dust hit the back of his throat. 'May, are you still there?' No answer. He pressed the redial button with his thumb and the screen lit up, 'No signal'.

He swore. He had to find a phone that worked. He had to talk to May. Tell her that he was a fool. That he was sorry. That he loved her... Always had. Always would. And he began to crawl forward, using the light from his phone to find his way.

May turned off the television. Pulled the plug out of the wall. It was the same thing over and over. Regional experts, former ambassadors, political pundits all saying nothing. Filling the airways of the twenty-four hour news channels day after day with the same lack of news told a thousand different ways.

That the fighting was fierce, that communications were limited to propaganda from government and rebel spokesmen. That casualties were high and that billionaire Adam Wavell, in Samindera to negotiate a major contract, was among those unaccounted for.

'Go out, Saffy,' she said. 'Take Nancie for a walk. Better still, go back to Paris and get on with your life. There's nothing either you or Michel can do here.'

She saw Robbie and Saffy exchange a look.

'May...'

'What?' she demanded. 'It's just another day.'

Not her wedding day. There was never going to be a wedding day.

That wasn't important.

She'd have surrendered the house, her business, everything she had just to know that Adam was safe.

She jumped as the phone rang but she didn't run to pick it up. She'd stopped doing that after the first few days, when she'd still hoped against hope that she was wrong. That he had somehow survived.

Now, each time she heard it, she knew it was going to be the news that she dreaded. That they'd found his body amongst the wreckage of one of those fancy hotels in the archive footage they kept showing.

Robbie picked it up. 'Coleridge House.'

She frowned, straining to hear, and then, without a word, she put the phone into her hand.

'May…'

The line was crackling, breaking up, but it sounded like…

'May!'

'Adam…' She felt faint, dizzy and Robbie caught her, eased her back into the chair. 'Are you hurt? Where are you?'

'God knows. The hotel…rebels…city. I'm sorry… wedding…'

She could barely follow what he said, the line was so bad, but it didn't matter. Just hearing his voice was enough. He was alive!

'Forget the wedding. It doesn't matter. All that matters is that you're safe. Adam? Can you hear me? Adam?' She looked up. 'The line's gone dead,' she said. Then burst into tears.

CHAPTER TEN

ADAM cursed the phone. He'd crawled through the blasted hotel liked the Pied Piper, using his phone to light the way, gathering the dazed and wounded, leaving them in the safety of the basement while he went to find water. First aid. Anything.

All he'd found were a group of rebels, who'd taken him with them as they'd retreated. He'd had visions of being held hostage for months, years, but as the government forces had closed in they'd abandoned him and melted away into the jungle.

He returned the useless cellphone to the commander of the government forces who'd finally caught up with them that morning.

'There's no signal.'

The man shrugged.

'How long before we get back to the capital?'

Another shrug. 'Tomorrow, maybe.'

'That will be too late.'

'There's no hurry. The airport is closed. The runway was shelled. There are no planes.'

'There must be some way out of here.'

The man raised an eyebrow and Adam took off his

heavy stainless steel Rolex, placed it beside him on the seat of the truck. Added his own top of the range cellphone, the battery long since flat. Then he took out his wallet to reveal dollars, sterling currency and tossed that on the pile. The man said nothing and he emptied his pockets to show that it was all he had.

'What is that?' the man asked, nodding at the tiny velvet drawstring pouch containing May's wedding ring. He opened it, took out the ring and held it up.

'If I'm not there,' he said, 'you might as well shoot me now.'

The silence after hearing from Adam was almost unbearable. To know that he was alive, but have no idea where he was, whether he was hurt...

May called Jake, called the Foreign Office, called everyone she could think of but, while the government was back in control, the country was still in chaos.

'Come on. It's your birthday tomorrow. I'm going to make a chocolate cake,' Saffy declared after breakfast.

'Can you cook?' She'd seen no evidence of it in the week since she'd arrived.

'Don't be silly. You're the domestic goddess. You'll have to show me how.'

Obviously it was in the nature of a distraction, but Saffy must be climbing the wall too, she realised.

They had just put it in the oven when the back door opened and Jake, not bothering to knock, tumbled through.

'Get your passport,' he said.

'Sorry?'

'Adam called. He's been driving through the jungle

for the last couple of days. He's in the back of beyond somewhere and it's going to take him at least three flights to get to the US. There's no way he can get home in time to beat the deadline, so you're going to have to go to him. I've booked you on a flight to Las Vegas—'

'Las Vegas?'

'You're getting married there, today.'

'But...' she glanced at the clock '...I can't possibly get there in time.'

'You're flying east. You'll arrive a few hours after you leave.'

'Yes!' Saffy said, jumping up and punching the air, grinning broadly.

'But...' She looked at Jake. Looked at Robbie, who was grinning broadly. 'I never bought a dress.'

'Forget the dress,' Jake said. 'You haven't got time to pack. We've barely got time to get to the airport.'

'What's the purpose of your visit to the United States, Mr Wavell?'

'I'm getting married today,' he replied.

The man looked him up and down. He'd been wearing his dinner jacket when the rebels had opened fire on his hotel. It was filthy, torn and there was blood on his shirt. It was scarcely surprising that he'd been pulled over at Immigration for a closer look.

'Good luck with that, sir,' he said, grinning as he returned his passport.

There was a driver waiting for him in the arrival hall.

'Miss Coleridge's flight is due in ten minutes, Mr Wavell,' he said, handing him an envelope containing a replacement cellphone and a long message from Jake detailing all the arrangements he'd made.

May paused as she entered the arrivals hall. Jake had told her she'd be met but she couldn't see her name on any of the cards. And then, with a little heart leap, she saw Adam and she let out a little cry of anguish. His clothes were filthy and torn, the remains of his shirt spattered with blood. He looked as if he hadn't slept for a week and he'd lost weight.

And his cheek… She put out her hand to touch a vivid bruise but he caught her hand. 'It's nothing. No luggage?' he asked.

'I didn't have time to pack. I didn't even have time to change,' she said, looking down at the smear of chocolate on her T-shirt. 'The wedding pictures should be interesting.' Then, keeping it light because it was all she could do not to weep all over him, 'But you know if you didn't want your mother to come to the wedding you only had to say. You didn't have to go to all this trouble.'

'I called her,' he said a little gruffly. 'Called Saffy. When I got to Dallas.' He cleared his throat. 'Dust,' he explained. 'From the explosion.'

'Adam…'

'Let's go. Apparently we have to get a licence at the courthouse before we go to the wedding chapel.'

'Well, that was easy,' May said as they walked out of the courthouse half an hour later with their licence. 'I hope, for your sake, that the divorce will be as simple.'

'Don't!' Then, seeing her startled look, realising that he had been abrupt, Adam shook his head.

He might have been seized by the sudden conviction that May was everything he'd ever wanted in a woman but she was doing this for only one reason.

To keep her home.

Crawling through the wreckage of the hotel, it had been the thought of May that had kept him going. The need to talk to her, tell her how sorry he was, what a fool he'd been. The hope that maybe they might, somehow, be able to begin again.

But, as the days had passed, all that had been swept away in the need to keep his promise to her. Because words meant nothing. No amount of sorry was worth a damn unless he backed it up with action.

Then, seeing the tiny frown buckling the space between her eyes, a frown that he wanted to kiss away, 'I'm sorry. I've had the worst week of my life and I vote that today we forget about everything, everyone else and just have some fun.'

'Fun?'

That was what he'd told Jake when he'd finally got to a phone that worked. To forget all the pompous nonsense he'd planned. He had, apparently, taken his brief very seriously. Instead of a simple limo, they'd been picked up at the airport in a white vintage open-topped Rolls, the kind that had great sweeping mud-guards, a wide running board, the glamour of another age.

Or maybe that *was* simple in Las Vegas.

'Any objections to that?' he asked, taking her hand as she stepped up into the car. Kept hold of it as he joined her.

'None.' May laughed out loud. 'I can't believe this. It seems unreal.'

'It is. Totally unreal,' he said, content to be sitting next to a woman wearing the biggest smile he'd ever seen. 'You've been given a magic day, stolen from the time gods by travelling east.'

'It doesn't work like that,' she said, leaning back against the soft leather, her hair unravelling, a smear of chocolate across her T-shirt. She looked exactly like the girl he'd fallen in love with, he thought, allowing himself to remember the heart-pounding edge as he'd climbed over the gate from the park. The heart lift as she'd looked up and smiled at him. He'd loved her before he knew the meaning of the word. And when he'd learned it was too late. 'I'll have to give it back when we fly home. You can't mess with time.'

'We give back the hours, but not anything that happens during them. You'll still be married. Your house will be safe. What we do, the memories we make. They are pure gain. That's why it's magic.'

She turned and looked at him. 'They should only be good memories, then.'

'They will be.'

'Seeing you in one piece is as good as it gets,' she said. 'I thought...'

May swallowed, turned away, tears clinging to her lashes. She'd promised herself she would not cry, but the shock of seeing him had been intense. She could not imagine what he'd been through while she was sitting in front of the television thinking that she was suffering.

She'd been so sure that the first thing she would do was tell him that she loved him. Worked out exactly what she was going to say on the long hours as she flew across the Atlantic, across America. But the moment she set eyes on him she knew that it was an emotional burden he didn't need. That she was doing what she'd accused him of. Thinking of herself. What she was feeling.

'Saffy was in bits,' she said when she could trust herself to speak.

'More than I deserve.'

Before she could protest, the car turned into a tropical garden and her jaw dropped as they swept up to the entrance to their hotel.

'Wow!' she said. Then, again, as they walked through the entrance lobby, 'Wow! This is utterly amazing.'

She was in Las Vegas and had expected their hotel to be large, opulent, over the top glitzy. But this was elegant. Stunningly beautiful.

'Good morning, Miss Coleridge, Mr Wavell. I hope you had a good flight?'

The duty manager smiled as he invited them to sit at the ornate Buhl desk, completely ignoring Adam's appearance. Her own.

'Just a few formalities. Miss Coleridge, you have an appointment at the beauty salon in half an hour,' he said, handing her an appointment card. 'We were warned that you would have no luggage and you'll find a selection of clothes in your size as well as your usual toiletries in your suite, as will you, Mr Wavell.'

She shook her head. 'Jake is great on the details,' she said. 'He thinks of everything.'

'You do have some messages, Mr Wavell. You can pick them up on voicemail from your room.' He looked from Adam to her and back again. 'Is there anything else I can do for you?'

'Just one thing,' Adam said. 'We're getting married

this afternoon. Miss Coleridge will need something very special to wear.'

'That's not a problem. We have a number of designer boutiques within the hotel and our personal shopper is at your disposal, Miss Coleridge. I'll ask her to call you.'

And Adam looked across at her with a mesmerising smile.

'Nearly everything,' he said.

The suite was beyond luxurious. A huge sitting room with wide curved windows that opened onto a private roof garden with a pool, a tiny waterfall, tropical flowers, a hot tub. There was an office, a bar, two bedrooms, each with its own bathroom.

There was also Julia, who introduced herself as their personal butler. While Adam picked up his messages, she had ordered a late breakfast for them, drawn them each a bath, and then unwrapped and put away their new clothes.

This is magic, May thought, sinking into the warm, scented water. She'd just closed her eyes when a phone, conveniently placed within reach so that she didn't have to move, rang once, twice. Was it for Adam? It rang again and she chided herself. This was the sort of hotel where if the phone rang in the bathroom it was for the person lying in the bath.

'Hello?'

'Good morning, Miss Coleridge. I'm Suzanne Harper, your personal shopper. I understand that you're getting married today and need something special to wear. Just a few questions and I'll get started.'

The few questions involved her colouring, style. Whether she preferred Armani, Chanel or Dior.

Dior! She couldn't afford that.

About to declare that she really didn't need anything, she thought of the way that Adam had looked at her as he'd said 'nearly everything'. He'd thought of this, arranged this. It was part of the magic and if she had to sell a picture to pay for it, it would be worth it.

'I don't have a particular preference for a designer. I'd just like something simple.'

That only left the embarrassing disclosure of her measurements.

'I'll go and see what I find,' she said thoughtfully. 'You'll be going down to the salon shortly?'

'My appointment's at twelve.'

'I'll bring a few ideas along for you to look at and we can take it from there.'

'Right.' Then, since she had the phone in her hand, she called home to let Robbie know that she'd arrived safely. Reassure Saffy that her brother was in one piece.

Adam looked up as May appeared wrapped in a heavy towelling robe, the partner of the one he was wearing, and smelling like heaven. 'Hi.'

'Hi,' she said, perching on the side of the desk. 'Everything under control?'

'Pretty much. How about you?'

'Well, I've just been through the mind-curdling embarrassment of giving every single one of my measurements to a woman I've never met.'

'Did she faint with shock?' he asked.

'She might have. There was a very long silence.'

'She was probably struggling to hold back a sob of envy that you have the confidence not to starve yourself to skin and bones.'

'I make sweets and cakes, Adam. I have to taste them to make sure I've got them right.'

'Your sacrifice is appreciated,' he said, holding out his hand to her and, when she took it, he pulled her down onto his lap, put his arms around her, and she let her head fall against his shoulder.

She'd pinned her hair up to get into the bath but damp tendrils had escaped, curling around her face. One of them tickled his chin and he smoothed it back, kissed it where it lay against her head. Saw a tear trickling down her cheek.

'Hey... What's the matter?'

'I thought you were dead.'

'I might as well have been if I'd let you down.'

'Idiot!' she said, throwing a playful punch at his arm.

'Ouch,' he said, covering his wince with a smile. 'Is that any way to speak to a man who's offering to show you a good time?'

She opened her mouth, closed it again. 'I'm so sorry, Adam. I thought this was going to be so simple.'

'It is, sweetheart. It is. But it's time you were moving,' he said before she became aware just how simple it was. Not even the thickness of the towelling robe could for long disguise just how basic his response to holding her like this had been. 'You'll be late for your appointment.'

She gave a little yelp, rushed off to the bedroom, returning a few minutes later in linen trousers the colour of bitter chocolate, a bronze silk shirt that brought out the colour of her eyes, her thick, wayward hair curling about her shoulders. The kind of hair that could give a man ideas. If he hadn't already got them.

'I'll meet you in the lobby at half past three.'

'In the lobby? But…'

'I'll finish up here, get ready and go out for a stroll in the garden.' He needed to put some distance between himself and temptation. 'You won't want me under your feet while you're getting ready.'

'Won't I?'

Without warning, her eyes hazed, darkened, an instinctive, atavistic response to what she must see in his; the kind of hot, ungovernable desire for a woman that he hadn't felt in longer than he could remember. The kind that set his senses ablaze, threatened to overwhelm him.

'Suppose I need a hand with a zip?'

'I only know how to undo them,' he said. A warning. As much to himself as to her. May trusted him. Believed his motives to be pure.

Not that she'd blame him. Knowing May, she'd almost certainly blame herself, apologise for taking advantage of him. He wasn't sure whether the thought of that made him want to smile, or to weep for her. A little of both, perhaps, and he wanted to hold her, tell her that she was amazing, sexy, beautiful and that any man would be lucky to have her.

She didn't move. Continued to stare at him, eyes dark, lips slightly parted, her cheeks flushed.

'May!'

She started. 'I'm gone.'

May wasn't sure what had just happened.

No. She wasn't that naïve. She knew. She just didn't know *how* it had happened.

How a jokey comment fired by nervous tension had

created a primitive pulse that made every cell in her body sing out to Adam, made every cell in his body respond to her so that the air shimmered like a heat haze around them. So that the rest of the room seemed to disappear, leaving him in the sharpest, clearest focus. His dark, expressive brows. The copper glints heating up his grey eyes. His mouth, lips that had kissed her to seal their bargain, kissed her again for no reason at all in a way that made her own burn just to think of them.

For a moment she leaned back against the suite door, weak to the knees with hot raw need, knowing that if he'd lifted a hand, touched her, she would have fallen apart.

And he'd known it, too.

He'd warned her. *'I only know how to undo them.'*

And, remembering just how adept he'd been with her shirt buttons, she didn't doubt it.

Even then she hadn't moved. Hadn't wanted to move.

All she'd wanted was him. To hold him in her arms. Know that he was safe. To show him with her body all the things that she couldn't say.

Adam could not remember the last time he'd felt the need for a cold shower.

He had fudged his promise when she'd asked if he intended a paper marriage. Lied with his heart, if not his tongue, planning an ice-cold seduction, determined that she should beg for him to take her.

But he knew that she had done nothing to hurt him. She had given him her heart, her soul, would have given him her body too, if they had not been discovered before his virgin fumblings had found the mark.

It had not taken a close call with death to teach him that there was no joy in revenge, only in life. He would marry May, then, as his captive partner for a year or so, living in the same house, he would woo her. Wait for her. Propose a real marriage when the false one was at an end.

But, while he could control his own desires, if May lit up like that again he wasn't sure he could fight them both.

May spent what seemed like an age in the salon. When she finally emerged, her unmanageable mess of mousy hair had been washed, trimmed and transformed. It was still mousy, but she was a very sleek, pampered mouse and her hair had gone up into a smooth twist, the only escaping tendrils those that had been teased out and twisted into well behaved curls.

The facial had toned and smoothed her skin to satin. The manicurist had taken one horrified look at her hard-working nails and transformed them with the application of acrylics. And someone she never actually got to see performed 'pedicure' on her feet, giving her toenails a French polish so exquisite that when she was ready to leave the salon, she felt guilty for putting her shoes back on.

And, all the while this had been happening, Suzanne had whisked outfits by her to gauge her reaction to style, colour, fabric.

Everyone had had an opinion and between them they'd whittled it down to four.

'That's the one,' Suzanne said when, back in their suite, she'd tried on an exquisite silk two-piece the warm, toasted colour of fine brandy. 'I knew it as soon as I saw your shirt. It's the perfect colour for you.'

'I do always feel good in it,' she admitted. 'Is it vulgar to ask the price?'

'I understood that Mr Wavell…'

'Mr Wavell is not paying for this.'

He'd already paid for a first class air fare, first class travel, the hotel, but that was all.

When Suzanne still hesitated—clearly the suit cost a small fortune—she said, 'Unless you tell me, Suzanne, you're going to have to take it back and I'll wear these trousers.'

She told her.

May did her best not to gulp, at least not noticeably. She wasn't going to have to part with some small picture by a minor artist, something she wouldn't miss. She was going to have to sell something special to pay for this. But she'd never look this good again and, whatever the sacrifice, it would be worth it, she decided, as she handed over her credit card.

'All of it, Suzanne. Shoes, bag, underwear, everything.'

'He's a lucky man.'

'I'm the lucky one,' she said, but more to herself than Suzanne and when, half an hour later, professionally made-up, dressed and ready to go, May regarded her reflection she couldn't stop smiling.

The skirt was a little shorter than she'd normally choose and straight, a style she usually avoided like the plague but it was so beautifully cut that it skimmed her thighs in a way that made them look sexy rather than a pair of hams. But it was the jacket that had sold her.

The heavy silk had been woven into wide strips to create a fabric that reflected the light to add depth to the colour. It had exquisite stand-away revers that crossed low over her breast. And, aided and abetted by the underwear that Suzanne had chosen, the shape emphasized rather than disguised her figure.

The final touch, the shoes, dark brown suede with cutaway sides, peep toes, a saucy bow and stratospherically high heels, would have made Cinderella weep.

'You look gorgeous, May. Go break his heart.'

CHAPTER ELEVEN

ADAM caught sight of himself in one of the mirrored columns and straightened the new silk tie he'd spotted in one of the boutiques.

Right now he knew exactly how a groom must feel as the minutes ticked by while he waited at the altar for a bride who wanted to give him a moment of doubt. A moment to face the possibility of life without her.

Doing his best to ignore the indulgent smiles of passing matrons who saw the spray of tiny orchids he was holding, the single matching orchid in his button-hole and drew their own conclusions, he checked his new wristwatch.

And then, as he looked up, she was there.

Hair messed up in a band incapable of holding it, wearing baggy sweats, spectacles propped on the end of her nose, May had managed to steal his heart.

Now, as their eyes met across the vast distance of the lobby, she stole his ability to breathe, to move, his heart to beat.

May was the first to move, lifting her feet with care in her high heels, moving like a catwalk model in the un-familiar clothes. Displaying her show-stopping ankles.

Heads turned. Men and women stopped to watch her. And then he was walking towards her, flying towards her, standing in front of her and, another first for him, he felt like a tongue-tied teenager.

'Nice flowers,' she said, looking at the spray of bronze-splashed cream orchids he was clutching. 'They really go with your tie.'

About to tell her that he'd chosen the tie, the flowers because they matched her eyes, he got a grip. 'Fortunately, they also match your suit,' he said, offering them to her.

'They're beautiful. Thank you,' she said, brushing a finger lightly over a petal, then lifting her fingers to the one in his buttonhole. 'You thought of everything.'

Nearly everything.

When he'd been clutching at straws, the last thought in his head was that he would fall in love with May Coleridge. He couldn't even say when it had happened. He'd spent the last hour wandering along the hotel's shopping mall, buying the tie, choosing flowers, looking at the yellow diamonds in Tiffany's window, trying to decide which shade would match her grandmother's engagement ring.

He took her hand, looked at it. 'I was going to buy you a ring.'

'I didn't mean...' She looked up. 'I was wearing it when Jake came for me.'

He shook his head. 'I don't think there's another ring in the world that would suit you more, so I bought this instead.' He took a small turquoise pouch from his pocket, tipped out a yellow diamond pendant. 'I think it matches.'

'Adam...' She put her hands to her cheeks as she blushed. 'I don't know what to say.'

'You don't say anything. You just turn around and let me fasten it for you.'

She might blush like a girl, he thought, as she did as she was told and he fastened the clasp at the nape of her lovely neck. But she lived her life as a mature, thoughtful, *real* woman.

One who'd worked at making a life, a future for herself, who might need a hand down once in a while when she'd climbed above her comfort level, but never looked to anyone else to prop her up.

He felt as if he'd been sleepwalking through his life. Putting all his energy, all his heart into building up his business empire, ignoring what was real, what was important.

He was awake now, he thought as he looked at May. Wide awake and tingling with the same anticipation, excitement as any of the other men who'd been queuing up for their wedding licences this morning.

'You look amazing.' Then, because he was in danger of making a fool of himself, 'I didn't mean for you to pay for it. The suit.'

'I know, Adam. But my grandmother once told me that when a man buys a woman clothes he expects to be able to take them off her.'

That had come out so pat that he knew she must have been rehearsing it for just this moment. A reminder…

'Your grandma was a very smart woman,' he said. 'I wish she was here to see what a lovely granddaughter she has.'

'Me too.' Then, with a sudden brightening of her eyes, 'Shall we go?'

He offered her his arm and, as they walked towards the door, there was a smattering of applause. The doorman whisked the car door open for them, raised his hat and then they drove out into the soft afternoon sunshine.

On the surface, May was calm, collected, knees braced, breath under control. It was the shoes that did it. Wearing heels that high required total concentration and while she was walking in them she didn't have a brain cell to spare for anything else.

The minute she slipped her hand under Adam's arm and she knew that if she tripped he'd catch her, everything just went to pot. He'd been in danger, hurt, tired, but he'd done this for her and, while the legs kept moving, everything else was just jelly.

'Are you okay?' he asked.

She nodded, not trusting herself to speak and then, just when she was absolutely sure she was going to hyperventilate, the car slowed and she saw the big sign and let out a little gasp.

'A Drive-thru Wedding?'

'You did say to let Jake surprise us,' Adam reminded her. Then he groaned. 'You hate it. I'm so sorry, May. This is all wrong. You look so elegant, so beautiful. Maybe it's not too late—'

'You deserve something more than this, May. Something special. The hotel have a wedding chapel. Maybe they can fit us in—'

'No!' He looked so desolate that she took his hand in hers, all the shakes forgotten in her determination to convince him. 'This is absolutely perfect,' she assured him. 'I love it.'

And it was true; she did. It was sweet. It was also as far from anything she could ever have imagined as possible. A wedding to make her laugh rather than cry. Nothing solemn about it. Nothing to break her heart.

'I love it,' she repeated.

I love you...

The minister, dressed in a white suit, was waiting at the window. 'Miss Coleridge? Mr Wavell?'

'Er, yes...'

'Welcome to the Drive Thru Wedding Chapel. Do you have your licence?' he asked.

Adam took it from his jacket pocket, handed it over for him to check it.

'Are you both ready to take the solemn vows of matrimony?'

He looked at her.

'Absolutely,' she said quickly.

He turned to Adam, who said, 'Positively.'

They said their vows without a hitch. Adam slipped her grandmother's ring onto her finger. Opened his palm for her to take the second plain gold band, exactly like hers, only much larger.

It was as if the whole world was holding its breath as she reached for it, picked it up, slipped it onto his finger.

'I now pronounce you man and wife. You may kiss the bride.'

'May I kiss the bride, Mrs Wavell?' he asked.

She managed to make some kind of sound that he took for yes and, taking her in his arms, he touched his lips to hers in what began as a barely-there kiss but deepened into something that melted her insides and might have lasted for ever but for the command from the photographer to hold that for one more.'

They collected the pictures, along with the souvenir certificate of their wedding vows at the next window.

'Photographic evidence,' he said, glancing through them, offering her a picture of them kissing with the Drive Thru Wedding sign behind them. 'Maybe we should send it to *Celebrity*?'

'Set a new trend in must-have weddings, you think?'

'Maybe not. But it should keep Freddie happy until Jake has organised all the legal registrations.'

She nodded, then said, 'There's just one more thing.' He waited. 'Where are the burger and fries?'

'I'm sorry?'

'A drive thru wedding should have a drive thru wedding breakfast.'

'You're hungry?' he asked.

'Hollow.'

She'd been so wrapped up in taking care of her grandfather, the house, keeping her mind occupied with the workshops. Never giving herself a moment to think. She was, she'd discovered, starving, but not for food.

The emptiness went far deeper than that.

She was hungry for Adam to look at her as he had in their suite. To touch her. To touch him. To kiss him, be his lover as well as his friend. Yearned for his child to hold. To be, if only for a magic afternoon, his wife in every sense of the word.

'I don't know whether it's lunch time, dinner time or breakfast time,' she said a touch light-headedly, but I haven't eaten since I left the plane and you should know that I'm not a woman who's accustomed to subsisting on a lettuce leaf.' She turned as they passed a familiar logo. 'There! We could drive in there and pick up a cheeseburger and some fries.'

He grinned. 'You are such a cheap date, May.'

'Hardly. You've already paid for a first class air fare,

a hotel suite fit for a prince and a diamond pendant.' She touched the diamond where it lay in the hollow of her throat. 'It's clear that you need a wife to curb your extravagance. But I will want a strawberry milkshake.'

They were laughing over their impromptu picnic as they arrived back in their suite.

Julia, undoubtedly warned of their return by the front desk, was waiting for them with champagne on ice, a tray of exotic canapés, chocolates, a cake. And a basket of red roses so large that it seemed to dominate the huge room.

May went white when she saw them.

'Could you take those away, Julia?' she managed. 'I'm allergic to roses.'

'Of course, Mrs Wavell. Congratulations to you both.'

'Thank you.'

That was Adam. She couldn't speak. Couldn't look at him. Didn't move until she felt his hand on her shoulder.

'It's okay, May. I know.'

'Know?' She looked up at him. 'What do you know?'

'About the rose petals.'

She stared at him, scarcely daring to breathe.

'What do you know?' she whispered.

'I know that you gathered them up and pressed them between the pages of a poetry book.'

Gathered them up. That made it sound like something pretty. But it hadn't been pretty, any of it. She'd crawled around on her hands and knees in the dark, slipping where the water had frozen, refusing to give up until she had them all. She couldn't pick them up in gloves and her hands had been so cold that she hadn't felt the scrapes, the knocks.

'How? No one knew…'

'I picked it up when I was waiting for you in your sitting room. A petal fell out. I didn't realise the significance until later, when I understood what you'd done for Saffy. That was why I called you the second time. You saved my life. If I'd been in bed instead of sitting on the floor talking to you…'

'He gave me a choice,' May said quickly, not wanting to hear how close she'd come to losing him. Not when he was here, safe. 'Swear that I would never speak to you, contact you, ever again. Or Saffy would go to jail.'

'But once she'd been cautioned…'

'I gave my word. He kept his.' She lifted her hands to his face, cupping it gently. Kissed the bruise that darkened his cheekbone. 'Forget it, Adam. It's over.'

'How can it ever be over?' he said. 'It was your face that kept me going when I was crawling through that hotel. The thought of you…'

She stopped his words with a kiss, then slowly began to unfasten her jacket.

'What are you doing?'

'Making up for lost time,' she said, letting it drop. 'Taking back what was stolen from us.' She unhooked her skirt, hesitated, looked up and her eyes, liquid bronze beneath long dark lashes, sent a charge of heat through him that wiped everything from his brain. 'Any chance of some help with the zip?'

Never taking his eyes from her face, he lowered the zip and then, as the skirt slithered to the floor, he left his hand on the warm curve of her hip as he lowered his lips to hers.

It was as if they were eighteen again. Teenagers, touching each other, awed by the importance of it, realising that this was a once and forever moment that would change them both.

This was how she'd been then. Lit up. Telegraphing what she wanted with eyes like lamps. She'd been both shy and eager. Naïve and bold. Innocent as a baby and yet knowing more than he did. Knowing what she wanted. What he wanted. Slowing everything down, making him wait, making him feel like a god…

She was doing it now. Unfastening the buttons of his shirt as she backed him towards the bedroom, pushing it off his shoulders. Kissing each bruise she uncovered with a little groan until he bent and caught her behind the knees.

Lost in the heat of her kisses, the pleasure of her touch he felt reborn, made over until, her tiny cries obliterating everything but one final need, he was poised above her to make her, finally, his.

'Please, Adam,' she begged as he made her wait. 'Please…'

And in those three words his world shattered.

He rolled away from her, practically throwing him from the bed in his shame, his desperation to escape what he'd so nearly done.

It took May a moment to gather herself, but then, concerned that after his ordeal he was sick, hurt, she grabbed a robe, found him slumped in a chair, his head in his hands.

'What is it? Darling, please.' She knelt at his feet. 'Are you hurt? Sick?'

'No.'

She sat back on her heels. 'Tell me.'

'I was going to make you beg.'

She frowned, took his hand, but he pulled it away.

'I was going to make you beg. Take you in your grandfather's bed.' He looked up. 'When you told me you were going to lose your house, do you think I was touched with concern? I was cheering. I had you. I was going to wipe out the Coleridge name with my own. Parade you as Mrs Adam Wavell, the wife of the kid from the sink estate. Take you in your grandfather's bed and make you beg.'

'So, what are you saying? That I didn't beg hard enough?' she asked. 'Or do you want to wait until we get home? Do it there?'

His head came up.

'No! No…' He shook his head. 'I was wrong. I don't deserve you, but I thought if I waited, wooed you, showed you that I was worthy of you, maybe, at the end of the year, when you could be free if you wanted to be, I could ask you then to marry me properly.'

'A year?'

'As long as it takes. I love you, May. I've never wanted another woman the way I wanted you. Want you.'

'No.' She shook her head. Stood up. Took a step back.

'I spent a week of agony thinking you were dead. Regretting that I hadn't told you how much I love you when I had the chance. And then, idiot that I was, I decided not to burden you with my emotional needs. Well, here it is. I understand why you felt the way you did, but I've waited more than ten years for you to finish what you started, Adam Wavell.' She untied the belt of the robe she'd thrown about her. Let it drop to the ground. 'I'm not prepared to waste another year. How about you?'

She held out her hand, held her breath for what seemed like forever before he reached out, took it, then pulled her to him.

The bell-ringers were waiting to give it everything they had. The choir was packed with angel-voiced trebles and, behind May, the church was crowded with everyone she knew. And lots of people she didn't but planned to in the future. Freddie was there. Adam's mother. Saffy with Michel and his parents, Nancie decked out in pink frills as an honorary bridesmaid. Robbie, standing as her matron of honour.

It was exactly as she'd imagined it all those years ago. Every pew end decorated with a knot of roses, myrtle and ivy. The bouquet of bronze David Austin roses she was carrying, one taken for Adam's buttonhole.

Nearly as she'd imagined. Not even the celebrated local designer, Geena Wagner, could squeeze her into a dress her usual size. The truth was that one of her seamstresses had been working on her gown as late as last night—letting it out half an inch around the waist to accommodate the new life she and Adam had created on their impromptu honeymoon.

Exactly as she'd imagined and totally different. What she hadn't known as a teenager was how she would feel.

That dream had been the yearning for triumph of an unhappy girl. Make-believe. Window-dressing.

Today it was real and as she and Adam stood before the altar and the vicar began to speak... 'Dearly beloved, we are gathered here today to bless the marriage of May and Adam Wavell...' the overwhelming emotion was that of joy, celebration of a blessed union, of love given and received.

Coming Next Month

Available August 10, 2010

#4183 MAID FOR THE SINGLE DAD
Susan Meier
Housekeepers Say I Do!

#4184 THE COWBOY'S ADOPTED DAUGHTER
Patricia Thayer
The Brides of Bella Rosa

#4185 DOORSTEP TWINS
Rebecca Winters
Mediterranean Dads

#4186 CINDERELLA: HIRED BY THE PRINCE
Marion Lennox
In Her Shoes...

#4187 INCONVENIENTLY WED!
Jackie Braun
Girls' Weekend in Vegas

#4188 THE SHEIKH'S DESTINY
Melissa James
Desert Brides

LARGER-PRINT BOOKS!

GET 2 FREE LARGER-PRINT NOVELS PLUS
2 FREE GIFTS!

HARLEQUIN® Romance®

From the Heart, For the Heart

YES! Please send me 2 FREE LARGER-PRINT Harlequin® Romance novels and my
2 FREE gifts (gifts are worth about $10). After receiving them, if I don't wish to receive
any more books, I can return the shipping statement marked "cancel." If I don't cancel,
I will receive 6 brand-new novels every month and be billed just $4.34 per book in the
U.S. or $4.99 per book in Canada. That's a saving of 17% off the cover price! It's quite a
bargain! Shipping and handling is just 50¢ per book.* I understand that accepting the 2
free books and gifts places me under no obligation to buy anything. I can always return
a shipment and cancel at any time. Even if I never buy another book from Harlequin, the
two free books and gifts are mine to keep forever.

186/386 HDN E7UE

Name _____ (PLEASE PRINT)

Address _____ Apt. #

City _____ State/Prov. _____ Zip/Postal Code

Signature (if under 18, a parent or guardian must sign)

Mail to the **Harlequin Reader Service:**
IN U.S.A.: P.O. Box 1867, Buffalo, NY 14240-1867
IN CANADA: P.O. Box 609, Fort Erie, Ontario L2A 5X3

Not valid for current subscribers to Harlequin Romance Larger-Print books.

**Are you a current subscriber to Harlequin Romance books and want
to receive the larger-print edition? Call 1-800-873-8635 today!**

* Terms and prices subject to change without notice. Prices do not include applicable
taxes. N.Y. residents add applicable sales tax. Canadian residents will be charged
applicable provincial taxes and GST. Offer not valid in Quebec. This offer is limited to
one order per household. All orders subject to approval. Credit or debit balances in a
customer's account(s) may be offset by any other outstanding balance owed by or to the
customer. Please allow 4 to 6 weeks for delivery. Offer available while quantities last.

Your Privacy: Harlequin Books is committed to protecting your privacy. Our Privacy
Policy is available online at www.ReaderService.com or upon request from the
Reader Service. From time to time we make our lists of customers available to
reputable third parties who may have a product or service of interest to you.
If you would prefer we not share your name and address, please check here. ☐

Help us get it right—We strive for accurate, respectful and relevant communications.
To clarify or modify your communication preferences, visit us at
www.ReaderService.com/consumerchoice.

HRLP10R2

HARLEQUIN®

A *Romance*

FOR EVERY MOOD™

Spotlight on

Heart & Home

Heartwarming romances
where love can happen
right when you least expect it.

See the next page to enjoy a sneak peek
from Harlequin® American Romance®,
a Heart and Home series.

CATHHHAR10

Five hunky Texas single fathers—five stories from Cathy Gillen Thacker's LONE STAR DADS *miniseries. Here's an excerpt from the latest, THE MOMMY PROPOSAL from Harlequin American Romance.*

"I hear you work miracles," Nate Hutchinson drawled. Brooke Mitchell had just stepped into his lavishly appointed office in downtown Fort Worth, Texas.

"Sometimes, I do." Brooke smiled and took the sexy financier's hand in hers, shook it briefly.

"Good." Nate looked her straight in the eye. "Because I'm in need of a home makeover—fast. The son of an old friend is coming to live with me."

She was still tingling from the feel of his warm palm. "Temporarily or permanently?"

"If all goes according to plan, I'll adopt Landry by summer's end."

Brooke had heard the founder of Nate Hutchinson Financial Services was eligible, wealthy and generous to a fault. She hadn't known he was in the market for a family, but she supposed she shouldn't be surprised. But Brooke had figured a man as successful and handsome as Nate would want one the old-fashioned way. *Not that this was any of her business…*

"So what's the child like?" she asked crisply, trying not to think how the marine-blue of Nate's dress shirt deepened the hue of his eyes.

"I don't know." Nate took a seat behind his massive antique mahogany desk. He relaxed against the smooth leather of the chair. "I've never met him."

"Yet you've invited this kid to live with you permanently?"

"It's complicated. But I'm sure it's going to be fine."

Obviously Nate Hutchinson knew as little about teenage

boys as he did about decorating. But that wasn't her problem. Finding a way to do the assignment without getting the least bit emotionally involved was.

Find out how a young boy brings Nate and Brooke together in THE MOMMY PROPOSAL, coming August 2010 from Harlequin American Romance.

HAREXP0810

THE HEAT IS ON
by
Jill Shalvis

The attraction between Bella and
Detective Madden is undeniable.
But can a few wild encounters
turn into love?

Don't miss this hot read.

*Available in August
where books are sold.*

---

red-hot reads

www.eHarlequin.com

*A powerful dynasty,
eight daughters in disgrace...*

Absolute scandal has rocked the core of the infamous
Balfour family. The glittering, gorgeous daughters are in
disgrace.... Banished from the Balfour mansion, they're
sent to the boldest, most magnificent men
to be wedded, bedded...and tamed!

And so begins a scandalous saga of dazzling glamour
and passionate surrender.

Beginning August 2010

MIA AND THE POWERFUL GREEK—*Michelle Reid*
KAT AND THE DAREDEVIL SPANIARD—*Sharon Kendrick*
EMILY AND THE NOTORIOUS PRINCE—*India Grey*
SOPHIE AND THE SCORCHING SICILIAN—*Kim Lawrence*
ZOE AND THE TORMENTED TYCOON—*Kate Hewitt*
ANNIE AND THE RED-HOT ITALIAN—*Carol Mortimer*
BELLA AND THE MERCILESS SHEIKH—*Sarah Morgan*
OLIVIA AND THE BILLIONAIRE CATTLE KING—*Margaret Way*

8 volumes to collect and treasure!
